Guilty Pro

By

Mark Farley

@mfarleyauthor

'For Suzanne and Alice'

Cover and Illustration created by my talented cousin, **Luke Farley**.

More of his work can be found at the following;

Lukefarleyillustration.com

Insta: @farley.luke

Acknowledgements

CHAPTER 1

Their hands clasped together in the moist spring air. The bitter snap of the south facing wind forced the couple to tighten their fingers and interlock their arms.

Early springtime in rural Alice Hills was generally colder than the rest of England. As a secluded village with open landscape in Northern England it wasn't surprising that the Winter months crossed with Spring. Wikipedia describes Alice Hills as a 'quaint and delightful village - Beautiful views with peaks and forestry to die for'. It's a regular rambling hotspot and attracts plenty of dog walkers and bird watchers.

The damp undergrowth softened the footsteps of the linked armed lovers. A squelching ice laced puddle broke the silence of the woodland every few metres. Wearing expensive wellies and waterproof trousers was a good choice on this particular Monday morning. Matching bobble hats and gloves was a sign to any passers-by that they were a committed couple in the early stages of their relationship.

"Morning," a local dog walker greets the young couple. There was no verbal reply, but the pair reciprocated with gleaming smiles. They follow up with a sigh and exhale of the crisp air as the dog hurtles and fades away into the coppice. The condensation from their deep breath's clouds their vision momentarily as they approach a stile.

"Here, give me your hand," the male helped the female over the stile with some dignity.

"Thanks, babe."

The early morning sun was limiting the possibility long distance views for the couple. Placing their gloved hands above their eyebrow gave them a quick opportunity to prepare their route and general direction.

"Dog shit, again!"

"No respect, these dog walkers."

It was like a game of hopscotch through the woods towards the Pike – clambering through rock laden pathways and stiles were not for the faint hearted. Dog poo was just another obstacle to walk around. The Pike was the pinnacle of Alice Hills. It could be seen from miles away. Mountains aside, it was one of the highest points in the country and gave breath taking views as far as the eye could see. It was a like ghost town at the peak of the Pike, too extreme for amateurs and dog walkers. Many people didn't venture as far as the summit.

The couple took a seat on the grassy area besides the Pike and opened their dual buckled backpack. A flask of coffee and some lukewarm bacon sandwiches wrapped in tin foil sat abreast a couple of bananas. It was a beautiful moment, the nearest road was at least three miles away, only the sounds of birds could be heard. Well, between the crumples of the tin foil anyway. It was a little windy and brisk but, an outdoor breakfast in the winter-come-spring elements beats being cooped up in the grotty café in town.

"So, what's the plan?" she asked with a mouthful of bread.

"Ow!" the male voice replied as he rushed to gulp the coffee. "Yep, I've just scolded my mouth."

He scratched his chin, deep in thought as he knew exactly what she was asking about. His delay in responding confirmed to her that he was trying to think of something to change the subject. She was smitten and gazed lovingly into his eyes as she tried to encourage him to speak. The outdoors always provides the opportunity for deep thinking and planning. There was no reason to rush conversation.

"Another time, let's enjoy this," he mustered up a brave response. "Look, a Deer," he quickly tried to change the subject.

The mood changed drastically, and she shuffled away from him, not without taking a further bite of her sandwich though. She muffled, "look, just make a decision."

A dark cloud could be seen in the distance. A signal to move on. The lid was popped back on the flask and the tin foil waste was screwed up into a golf sized ball and put into the backpack.

"Up we get!"

Zips were pulled up, wellies straightened out and the gloves wrapped up their cold hands. The dire mood didn't last long. They soon held hands again and headed in the direction of the rising sun. It was downhill from now on, a gradual slope led through to the same woodland they had been in before.

"Just watch your footing, love."

They briefly parted hands whilst trying to tackle the obstacle course of rocky boulders and sloppy mud. Entering back into woodland provided shelter from the wind, a welcome rest bite.

There was a huge bang in the distance. "What was the that?" the female voice was shaken.

The male placed his hand across his eyebrow again. The sun was breaking through the twiggy trees causing broken beams of light to hinder the view.

"I can't tell from here. I heard something too though."

A horse bolted out from the overgrowth at great speed and briefly startled them both – causing them to get safety behind a huge oak tree. They both looked around noticed a gap in the barbed wire fence, the horse must have broken free from the local farm grounds. The female grabbed the arm of her companion with a sigh of relief. A considerable amount of time had passed since they left the Pike and it had been at least an hour or so since they left home. The crunching sound of fallen branches was intermittent between the scurrying footsteps of squirrels and singing birds. Bliss. Not another human in sight which was the whole point in these quiet morning walks. This side of the Pike was always pleasant with wildlife as few people would come to this area of Alice Hills, only experienced and local walkers would go off the beaten track to explore.

"I love our Monday morning walks."

"Me too. What's that?" The male replied.

"Now It's your turn to be scared," she joked.

There was silhouette in the distance. A lone person in dark clothing. The rays of sunlight limited the view of the approaching figure. The shock of the earlier noise and the uncommon event of another person on this side of the Pike made for an eerie moment. Time passed, slowly, as the couple neared the approaching loner. Each squelch of mud and crack of sticks loudened and heightened the atmosphere. Birds had stopped tweeting and squirrels could no longer be seen. What aura was this mystery person carrying?

The broad shoulders outline a man as the view became clearer. A black hooded jacket zipped up past the chin was matched with a low riding baseball cap. Waterproof trousers adorned with so called fashionable zips were paired with distinctive orange outdoor boots.

It was a muffled but pleasant greeting from the stranger as he passes the walking couple, "Good morning."

A wry smile in response is all the pair could muster up.

"See, scared and tension building for nothing," the male scorns the female.

A quick check over her shoulder eases the atmosphere, the man carried on walking.

"Who dresses like that?" she stammers.

"It's about 2 degrees, love," he laughed. "At least he acknowledged us."

She pouted her lips and raised her eyebrows with a follow up nod of the head. The international signal of 'erm, yea, maybe'.

The scenery of the woods allowed the freedom of thought. There were no distractions, and it was evident that the couple could embrace the budding flowers of Spring and forget about life's troubles. They approached a fallen tree, a large fir tree which must have been a victim of the harsh 2017 Winter. It was clearly rotten; the bark was crumbling, and insects had set up camp. England was rocked in 2017 by its harshest ever recorded Winter. These were the real effects of Global Warming and the elements didn't let Alice Hills off lightly. Buildings were blown down, trees were carried for miles and that was before the ten feet of snow set in for a couple of months.

The male shrugged his shoulders at the sight of the lying tree.

"Easy," the female quipped.

She hurdled the tree like a young Lebron James making a slam dunk. A graceful leap with a perfect landing. He was impressed with the elegance and flair but he needed a confidence builder. She laughed like an innocent young girl as he mockingly took strides in a backwards position, imitating a long jumper at the Olympics. He raised his hands above his head, slightly knocking his hat over his eyes and he started to clap. His front foot splurged some mud over the laces of his boots as he prepared to ignite.

"Go, go, go," she shouted.

The right arm of the male was thrown in front of him and he leapt into a sprint. One step, two steps, three steps. The female had her hands over her face, she could barely focus.

THUD!

At first, she thought he had fallen. His mother would always call him a klutz so it wouldn't be a shock. She gently pulled her hands away from her eyes and brushed the stray hair to one side. He was on the floor. In a panic, she straddled the fallen tree and climbed over. No hurdling this time. She called his name several times but there was no response. More panic set in as she rushed in on her knees, sliding through the mud. It was clear he had a head injury; blood had seeped through the woolly hat. The injury was to the back of his head and he was lying face down, suffocating within the sludge.

With her tiny frame she used all of her strength to flip his body over. Between the calls of his name she muttered, 'How? Why?'. Whilst in a fluster, a million thoughts rushed through her head. His eyes were closed and there was no sign of life. She glanced longingly over her left and right shoulder for help between each mouth to mouth resuscitation and chest compression.

She staggered to her feet; her gloves were covered in blood. Deep and frantic breaths echoed through the silence of the woods.

"Help!" She screamed, frightening local wildlife into a frenzy.

A man appeared, as if from nowhere. She recognised the orange boots as her eyes looked up and down his towering body. It was the same man from before and she struggled to work out what was going on. She glanced down to her partner for support, but he had not risen. It was too late, she could do no more. The strange man wasn't there to help, and her confusion morphed into the stark reality of what had really happened and what was going to happen next.

Her flailing body was thrown back over the fallen tree and the stranger pulled out a blood-stained baseball bat. Hurt from the fall, she stiffened up with dread. The baseball bat streamed with blood, a memoir from the last victim. The attacker positioned himself over her legs and kicked out at his bat as though he was preparing for a pitch in the World Series. His arms raised up, this was going to be a home run.

The bat came down with a frightful force and struck the head. Darkness.

CHAPTER 2

"I can see clearly now the rain has gone."

Bang!

A sleepy hand slapped the button of the alarm and turned it off before the bed covers were pulled over to one side. The hairy feet of a male scrunched into the carpet and his clammy hands rubbed his eyes.

"That was the most vivid dream I have ever had," he croaked. "I should probably class that as a nightmare actually."

"Matt, go back to sleep. It's Monday," a tired female voice replied.

Helen was accustomed to her husband's dark sense of humour and lack of empathy, so she wasn't one for giving him any bait.

"I'm in work today anyway. What you on about having a lie in for?" Helen didn't reply but it didn't stop Matt from elaborating. "This dream. I've just dreamed about a savage beating up in Alice Hills... so surreal."

Matt leant in with his morning breath and kissed Helen's silky brown hair. He would often say that she was at her most beautiful first thing in the morning with her flawless skin and athletic body. They were both nearing forty years old, but Helen didn't look a day over twenty five. Matt on the other hand had inherited his father's receding hairline.

Helen bit the bait, so much for trying to ignore him. "Go on, what did they look like?"

"No idea, well I can't remember," Matt coughed.

Helen raised her eyebrows as she popped her slippers on. She clearly wasn't impressed with the lack of detail in Matt's 'surreal and vivid dream'.

"It's been years since we've been up there. Alice Hills. We'll have to make a trip of it next weekend," Helen said.

Helen made her way to the en-suite bathroom whilst Matt headed down the spiral stairs of their 1920's home to make breakfast. They were both awake slightly earlier than usual for a Monday. Matts restless night of sleep being the likely culprit. Helen was a lawyer who worked from home twice a week, so she was in no rush to get ready.

Cooking a wholesome breakfast was usually a weekend treat but the early wakeup gave Matt the opportunity to express his inner chef. It also gave him some time to dwell further into his dream. The cracking of the egg created a flashback to the sound of the baseball bat striking the head. Matt staggered in a circle and held his head as he cracked the second egg. A blinding surge of pain created a blistering headache.

The white of the egg splashed across the hob of the cooker before Matt rushed up the stairs. He staggered and banged off the wall and the adjacent bannister.

"Are you ok?" Helen screams with concern from the shower.

Matt spewed into the toilet bowl, "painkillers please."

A naked Helen jumped from the behind shower screen and resulted in a makeshift ice rink in the bathroom. Beige and glitter floor tiles did make for a beautiful and modern bathroom though. Helen raided the cabinet, knocking out age-old soaps from Christmas's gone by, trying to locate the multitudes of paracetamol boxes that she thought they had.

"Bloody hell, why are they are at the back," she ranted.

Helen ripped open a box of painkillers and put two pills into Matts mouth. Emptying the toothbrushes, she filled up the holder with water before Matt washed painkillers down. He was sweating. His grey logo themed top was drenched, but he was grateful for the over reactive rampage his wife had just endured whilst he slumped on top of the toilet seat.

"Thanks, you can jump back in the shower now," a slight tap to the bum to nudge her away was enough to make Helen realise he was ok.

"What was all that about?" Helen was back to washing her hair.

"It was a flashback to that dream I mentioned. Bizarre," he glanced into the mirror and rolled his lower eye lids down.

The washing of her hair gave Helen the delayed time she wanted to avoid a response. Saved by the bell. The smoke alarm went off. "Shit."

There was no time for Matt to recover or wait for his wife's response. He rushed out of the bathroom, scrambling past the clutter along the landing before slipping down the stairs. The loud crashing noise alerted Helen again.

"You ok?" The lack of empathy in her voice indicated that he had done this before.

An unconvincing sigh and follow up response, "Yea."

"I told you to move that..."

"Stuff. I know, I know," Matt muttered.

The smoke alarm was still blaring out, but Matt managed to move the pan with the burnt eggs to one side. A quick flurry of the tea towel round the kitchen shifted the smoke to the open window. Not quite perforated but slightly numb, his ears received a welcome ambience when the smoke alarm turned off. Along with his pride, he realised his neck and shoulder was hurt too. His sweat stained top had now been diluted with blood from a laceration to his shoulder area.

"I must have caught myself on the bannister," he mumbled to himself.

He took his top off, but the cut had pretty much stopped bleeding. Helen was making her way down the stairs, so he quickly dabbed the cut and threw on a nearby shirt from the fresh laundry. Matt didn't need the extra embarrassment of a cut to add to the list of calamities and concerns.

"It's a good job you're at your brothers today, he can look after you," Helen scoffed as she bit into a banana.

Matt was puzzled. He was sure this was a working day.

"You're off work to help him fit a new shed," Helen gave a less than impressed look.

Matt sheepishly nodded and smiled, "I know, just testing." The stumble on the stairs had given him a bigger knock than initially thought.

The relationship between Matt and Helen was strong but they would often take each other for granted. An outsider would suggest that the forgetfulness of both of their whereabouts was showing a lack of interest but, Matt would often argue it was a mark of respect and trust. 'I don't need tabs on Helen' was a regular comeback comment down at the pub with the lads.

"You better go upstairs and get ready. I've got work to do and your brother is expecting you anytime now. I'll clean this mess up."

Matt snatched a slice of dry cold toast from the kitchen worktop and bit down on it to avoid a verbal reply. The creak of stairs on the way up was a sign of the buildings age but the rocking of the bannister showed the lack of upkeep on the interior.

Helen had already jumped into the office at the back of the house with a black coffee, two sugars. She was a real workaholic wanting to climb the career ladder at her firm. Matt felt like the firm was taking her for ride, eking every last minute of time out of her without any support or reward. Her parents felt the same as Matt. They wanted a grandchild and Helen was an only child. She was prioritising work life over family life. Helen was still young but as a thirty something career laden lady, she was bound by social pressures and her fertility clock. Helens maturity and intelligence would always prevail when the conversation of children came up. Forty was the new twenty in her strong set mind.

Fresh from the bathroom and pulling up his socks sat on the edge of the bed, Matt felt fresh and a world away from that earlier headache. He had time to think about his dream whilst in the shower, but no more information had been forthcoming. No faces, no voices... nothing. He hadn't been awake long but like every dream, the detail was fading as the day progressed. It was time to forget about it. A quick finger slide across the eyebrows and a flick of the hair towards the full-length mirror besides the bedroom door was a daily task. In fact, it was a ritual.

"See you later," Matt peered his head into the home office.

Helens hand popped up from behind the laptop and gently waved. The plug-in air freshener omitted a blast of lavender as Matt picked up his jacket and keys from the couch causing him to splutter. Helen, paranoid from all of his earlier mishaps double checked that he was okay. Matt's brother didn't live too far away but he wasn't exactly enthusiastic and in a rush about building a shed on his only day off work. The front door was sticky but with a forceful and upward lift Matt was out of the door, in the car and halfway down the long driveway.

CHAPTER 3

"I'm on my way."

"See you in a bit then."

It was a typical brotherly phone call. Straight to the point with no gossip. The sun shone low and brightly, forcing Matt to pull down the visor. A picture of him and Helen on their wedding day was pinned to the underside which always triggered a smile from Matt. The open roads on the outer skirts of Alice Hills were covered by overgrowing trees and open fields but, vehicles littered the area to make it look unsightly. It was only by going further away from the town area of Alice Hills that peace and serenity was an option.

The photograph of his wedding day distracted Matt and his hands on the steering wheel swung to the right as a blaring horn from an approaching truck beeped at him, "Whoa, bloody hell!"

His day dreaming would often get him into trouble but not usually in a physical fashion. It was a common occurrence at work or at home when somebody needed his attention; people would often have to repeat themselves. The near death experience was a new one for him.

Matt pulled over into a near layby. A quick glance into the mirror and over his shoulder reassured Matt that he was safe. The truck driver carried on into the distance but not before leaving a huge cloud of dust from the off-road swerving. The last thing he needed was a grilling from an oversized trucker. His brother would have had a field day had he seen this. Matt was often a butt of jokes due to his small slight frame and clumsiness, especially when they were both younger.

A quick respite and a rub of the eyes before sticking the indicator on was enough to bring back his confidence. The back of his brother's house could be seen from the layby but the coast was clear, nobody would have seen the near miss. Matt had his concentration face on until he reached the driveway of the house. His brother was already waiting for him. He looked like a nightclub bouncer as he leaned on the open doorway with his six foot something frame and his arms bulging from his short sleeved top. If he wasn't working on a building site, he was stuck in the gym. Image was everything to Josh. He even had a lengthy beard that would only be trimmed by the local Turkish barber.

"Some entrance that, brother," Josh laughed as he flexed his arms towards the road behind his house.

Matt slammed the door of his car behind him and sarcastically laughed back.

"Have you got nothing better to do but play the town voyeur?"

"Alice Hills Pike is in the background. I was enjoying the view with a brew when I heard the truck beeping his horn because of somebody on the wrong side of the road. It turns out that it was you. I bet you shit yourself."

Despite his larger frame, Josh still played the younger brother role well and cowered as Matt playfully jabbed away at his ribs as they walked through the doorway. But Josh soon came to his senses and got Matt in a headlock and rubbed his knuckles into his receding hairline.

Matt pushed him away and took a step towards the living room. It was a step too far and he started to get dizzy. With his eyes rolling back and his legs getting weary, Matt felt the room getting smaller. His peripheral vision started to narrow with a surrounding orb of blackness. The calls of his name from his brother, Josh, started to lower in tone and become duller. But, not as dull as the follow-up thud noise from Matt collapsing to the floor.

What seemed like an hour was probably about thirty seconds. The whole passage of dizziness and eventual collapse was supported by Josh. Josh sat Matt up against the wall as sweat streamed down his face in droves. The reassuring awakening of Matt allowed for Josh to dash to the kitchen for a large glass of water.

"Here, drink this."

Matt staggered to his knees, but Josh forced him back down to rest. Brotherly love wasn't lost after all. After a few minutes of silence and progressive composure, Josh helped Matt to his feet and led him to the back garden for some fresh air.

"There's the scene of tranquillity," Josh laughed and pointed to the road where the dust had only just begun to settle.

Matt laughed at his misunderstanding of the word tranquility. His sense of humour was still there so he must have been okay. The overcast sky allowed for a comfortable gathering in the garden. That was real tranquillity.

"What was all that about? Are you epileptic? It was only a small headlock," Josh quizzed Matt.

Matt wiped the last of the sweat away from his forehead with the sleeve from his shirt, "No. I don't think so anyway. It wasn't your headlock, I've just felt weird since waking up."

He hesitated and stopped mid-sentence. Matt wasn't confident in letting Josh know any detail of last night's dream so he held back on giving more details. Quick flashbacks went through his mind from their teenage years. A constant mickey taking from a younger and more masculine sibling in their youth was unbearable. Although, Josh had matured since adolescence, he didn't need many opportunities to give out a good humiliation. The near miss on the road earlier in the day proved that.

Pacing back and forth in the garden gave Matt the rush of blood and fresh air he needed. The adjacent area had been cleared out and his brother had already laid the foundations for the pending shed. It was still relatively early in the morning, so the birds were well into a rhythm of singing. It was a beautiful garden, a real sun trap with large grounds that attracted an assortment of wildlife. Josh was still stood towards the door on the patio with a surprising look of concern on his face.

"What do you think about the man cave space?"

The concern from Josh had changed and the shed began to take priority again. Matt turned around and placed his hand on his head to block out the sun through the clouds. "Man cave? I thought I was here to build a shed... Anyway, why do you need a shed and why do you need me... You're the builder."

Matt didn't take a breath. Borne of frustration and still reeling from his chaotic morning, Josh ignored him, laughed and headed back into the house to freshen up.

The cooling sweat had left a dry trail of body salt on Matts head so he also made his way back into the house. Not before looking over his shoulder at the pending man cave space. The fear and dread of the build was overpowering the dwindling fatigue from the blackout. There was a reason why Matt chose to be a car salesman. No manual labour involved. A bad knee injury as a child limited his career prospects but he often used it as an excuse to get out of doing things. He was more than capable of competing in running races and playing football, but any hard labour was not for him. Like a lot of people, Matt fell into his career rather than pursue it. His late father forced him to get a job or as he would say, *'get off his arse'*. Josh was his only brother and the grafter of the family, their father's golden child and Matt resented it.

Josh was making another coffee in the kitchen with the television on the background. He was smoking a cigarette and every drag was taking away an element of his soul. That's something else that their dad would say to Josh when he was younger. Matt couldn't recall the last time he saw Josh smoke, he thought he had quit a long time ago so he expressed a face of concern towards Josh.

"Don't worry, we're only laying the beams today. I know how much you hate hard work, but dad would have loved us working together," Josh laughed and stubbed out the cigarette. "That's why you're here. A bit of family time."

Matt was too distracted by the TV to pay any attention to his brother's comments, or the disposing of the cigarette end.

"Oi," Josh whistled and waved his hand in front of Matts face to click him out of the daze.

"Turn it up," Matt batted the hand of Josh away. He was focused on the TV; not daydreaming as Josh presumed. Josh couldn't be faulted for thinking otherwise. It was a well-known trait of Matt.

The voice of the news announcer blared out as Josh over excitedly turned his attention to the TV as well. Matt's glare and concentration confirmed that the optimal sound level was set.

"News just in. Details are still coming in, but a man has been found beaten in the nearby Alice Hills woodland by a local dog walker. His current situation, alive or dead, is not yet known. More to follow."

The voice was clean and eloquent. The words felt blunt and unsympathetic. Emergency access to the woodland would be complicated and the still images provided on the news report confirmed this. The blue tape surrounded the entrance at the back end of woods and tone of the images showed a couple of police officers clambering through a gate with some crime scene investigators. The media station had made the images grainy to add a distasteful effect, but it did set the tone of the occasion. An interval with commercials of reality TV exclusives soon brought back the social norm.

"They should hire bloody dog walkers in the police force," Josh quipped.

The awkward silence prompted Josh to continue, "It's always dog walkers that find bodies. They're bloody good investigators."

"Yes, I understood your point from the first remark."

"Well what's up then?" Josh slurped his coffee and took a seat at the table.

Matt sat across from him and scraped the chair forward along the tiled floor, "You'll only take the piss."

"I swear on dad's grave I won't."

"Too soon."

Their father had only died a few months ago and it was his dying wish that his two sons got along better and worked hard to maintain a close-knit family. Their father had outlived his wife, Matt and Josh's late mother, and with no grandchildren the family was getting smaller.

"I dreamed about somebody getting attacked in the those woods last night and I've felt uneasy ever since."

Josh let a little laugh out but a stern look from Matt prompted him to stop. It was a sharp schtum of the mouth, a natural understanding that the matter was serious. It was still awkward, and Matt was gathering his thoughts – too much information with no idea on where to start. Josh turned the TV off to ease the tension.

Matt paced around within the modern layout of the kitchen; his mind was trying to piece things together. He was counting the potential connections on one hand; not enough to carry on to the left hand.

"It's a bit blurry but I dreamed about two people walking through the woods over at Alice Hills and they were attacked by somebody."

"That's just a coincidence. I wouldn't go as far as saying you have premonitions. Just forget about it."

"I know, I know, but I was sick this morning and then I passed out as soon as I got here," Matt had sat back down and clasped his head in hands.

"Well, let us clear that head, Sunshine. Outside, now."

Josh was the joker of the family, always quick to ease an overwhelming atmosphere. His positivity radiated with whatever company surrounded him. On this occasion, it was his brother. Matt followed Josh into the garden, he still seemed to be suffering from shock but wanted to show strength. It was a typical male response and a positive trait that was instilled into the blood of their family DNA.

Matt spent a considerable amount of time pottering about in the garden trying to make sense of the ground works and what he was supposed to be doing. Whereas Josh got stuck straight into it.

"Shall I start at this end?" Matt asked and shuffled his way over to the opposite side of Josh, with a wooden beam in his hand.

"Josh, Josh. Hello," Matt was exasperated as he repeated himself over and over.

Matt gave up and just got on with what he thought he was right. The initial frustration of being blanked soon lightened as he thought about his own lack of communication. *Maybe he is just getting pay back for all of the times I drifted off into daydream land and ignored him*, Matt thought to himself.

Matt looked over to Josh, who was deep into taking dimensions with his tape measure and pencil. He loved his brother dearly and took a moment to embrace the time they were spending together.

Hours passed without much of a conversation between the two. The occasional break allowed for a cup of coffee, one too many in the opinion of Josh but he was being lenient to his apprentice. Warm weather slowed proceedings but the target of completing the decking floor by the afternoon was virtually achieved. There was no further mention of the dream or the earlier blackout. In fact, there was no real thinking about it. Matt had managed to get stuck in and surprise himself at how capable of manual work he really was. Maybe there was some potential hiding within his sedentary office bound body.

A creak of the rear garden gate put a stop to the intense labour. Matt and Josh simultaneously turned their heads down the long pathway towards the large wooden gate. It was Amy. Josh's girlfriend. She struggled through with bags of shopping but neither brother thought of helping. Josh turned back to work, and Matt drifted off into his own world, staring into no-man's land.

"Hello, Matt. Do you mind helping me with these bags?"

Matt didn't hesitate and rushed over grabbing as many of the bags that his weedy arms could carry. He struggled, but managed to get them inside the house without dropping any. *That seemed harder than the decking*, he thought, as he stretched his arms out.

"Matt!" Josh shouted. "Help me with this panel, will you!"

Matt shook his head and panned over to Josh – he was still in the garden. Checking back to the gate, he couldn't see Amy. She had progressed halfway through the back door and no longer needed any assistance. He stumbled over to Josh with weary legs and a hammer in his hand. The image of an apocalyptic zombie sprung to the mind of Josh but Matt could only think of the vivid day dream he had just had.

"What's wrong with you? I was shouting you for ages."

Matt steadied himself whilst grabbing the opposite end of the panel board from Josh, "Déjà vu or my mind went blank." Matt gave a self-confused look as his response made little sense, but he knew Josh would be none the wiser.

Josh thought about telling him to go to his doctor but held back knowing it would only make Matt more paranoid. He resorted to a shake of the head and pulled the panel harder making Matt concentrate more on the task at hand.

"I get that all the time," Josh tried to reassure his nervous brother realising he was being harsh.

The rest of the floor panelling didn't take long which was a huge relief for Matt. It did keep him occupied but his intrusive thoughts weren't kept at bay. Back in the house, Amy had put all of her shopping away and was relaxing in the living room with a book. The house was open plan so there weren't many places to hide, not that she was trying to do so. Amy was a quiet woman, early thirties and a similar age to Josh. Very beautiful with her long brown hair and Mediterranean olive skin. But her family and previous generations had no trace of anything but English DNA. Josh bought a family tree DNA kit for Christmas one time thinking that she had a far out and wide ancestry. It turned out that at least ten generations of her family lived no further than one hundred miles from where they currently lived. Some people are just blessed with good looks and perfect skin and Matt always thought his brother was a lucky man.

Matt was being nosy and sifted through the bookcase in the Kitchen. Amongst all the chick-lit, sport biographies and car manuals was a fertility book which grabbed his attention. "What's this?" he muttered.

A cloud of dust bloomed as Matt blew against the shelf and retrieved the book. The cough and splutter through the dust was enough to get his brothers attention who was filling a glass with water. A blushed and worried look came across the face of Josh.

Josh knocked over his glass and gave a panicked look as Matt wafted the dust away.

"Sorry, I didn't think there was that much dust. I'll clean it up," Matt was worried.

Matt put the fertility book down and paced towards the cleaning cupboard under the sink. "Where's your disinfectant?" The search for cleaning products gave Josh enough time to put the book back amongst the uncategorised collection of biographies. He needed to hide it, not that Matt noticed.

"Never mind, I've found it," Matt rushed back embarrassed at the mess he had made and started to clean up.

"Ninety-Nine-point nine percent of bacteria killed, eh. That nought point one dude is the real warrior we all need in our life," Matt was cracking jokes as a distraction.

Josh felt relieved as the attention was taken away from the book and any future awkwardness of discussing it. Josh glanced over to Amy rather worryingly. The scene was clear, she was still engrossed in her novel. It must be a good read to have missed all the chaos in the kitchen.

"She's quiet," said Matt as he put the cloth and cleaning products back in the cupboard.

"Yea..." Josh was leaning against the pillar as he adorned over Amy.

Matt was making simple conversation, but he knew that Amy was always quiet. She had a great personality; the problem was getting her to show it off.

"Anyway, I'm off. Give me a shout next week when you next need some help," Matt wanted to get out of the house after the scene he had caused.

"Help?" Josh laughed. "Only kidding. I will see you later in the week. You and Helen are around for dinner."

"Oh yea," Matt slapped his head at his forgetfulness.

Matt packed his pitiful excuse for a toolbox together and made his way to the front door. He couldn't help but notice an outfit hanging from the coat hanger near the door.

"What's this all about? You and Amy getting into role play?"

Matt picked up a pirate outfit which was incredibly detailed. Especially the beard. He rubbed his hands through the beard and got flash backs to his dream as his fingers weaved through the strands of hair. The level of detail on the beard was remarkable. Looking closely, Matt could barely see the underlining of how the hair was sewn in. The outfit was basic, but the beard was exceptional, and Matt stood there, stroking it. He was more intrigued with every brush through. *Did the attacker in my dream have a beard?* Matt thought about it but he just couldn't remember.

"Very funny and stop being weird," Josh snapped the outfit from Matt's hand. "It's Amy's from a fancy-dress party she went to over the weekend. Anyway, get going."

A quick nod to his brother signalled the departure. Saying bye to Amy on the way out didn't receive a response. She didn't even look up to acknowledge his presence. How ignorant, he thought. His feelings were kept to himself as he didn't want to upset his brother.

The journey back home was less eventful for Matt. A mundane trip up the local backtrack was a slight detour that was required to clear Matts head. The blacking out earlier in the day was a real shock and driving back the same way he came in wouldn't have been wise for his mental state. Trying to decipher the dream and consequential effects were overwhelming. The signals were telling Matt that he had a purpose. He was building a real desire to solve the crime in his dream and that of the one he saw the news. But were they the same?

The silence within the car interior was broken by a stomach rumble. It had been a long day and Matt was looking forward to dinner with Helen. Driving into his home street prompted the pulling down of the windscreen visor as the car headed towards the setting sun. It may have been in his mind, but Matt could swear that he could smell the home cooked meal from the window his car as he pulled onto the driveway. He was grateful and didn't want press judgment, but the food smelled like it was cooked in a school canteen. "I'm sure it'll be great," he whispered as he entered the house.

"Miss you, come back," a whimper was in Helens voice as she met Matt at the door.

"It's, missed. And, I am back," Matt smiled.

It was unlike Helen to do so but she stroked his slightly bearded face and kissed Matt, "you're a bit late but dinner is ready."

Matt reciprocated the greeting and then headed to kitchen to grab his dinner. Somehow it was still warm, no need for the microwave. Despite the smell, it looked like a Michelin Star meal, and this was typical of Helen. She had a real calling for producing high quality food, but it didn't explain why the odour was so rank. He was late home, so Helen had already eaten but it gave Matt the opportunity to grab a beer and eat in front of the TV. A luxury these days as Helen was always keen on them eating at the table for a conversation about their day.

Eating in front of the TV with a cold beer was just what Matt needed after the events of the day. It provided some time to zone out and get oxygen pumping to the brain. The TV didn't provide much use to Matt, he was an outdoor man but, it provided the right amount of background noise to drift off into another world when need for relaxation was called for.

He was barely into his seventh bite and the first set of commercials had started, but a real background noise caught Matt's attention. It was crying. They were the sounds of Helen crying. An overwhelming feeling of warmth and concern came over Matt. He placed the plate of the half-eaten steak to one side and manoeuvred through the house in an attempt to find Helen. His calls for Helen were not receiving a response. Nobody was downstairs and there was no sense of what direction the sobbing was coming from. The sound wasn't getting any closer, but it wasn't getting further away either. It was the warmth of Helen that was helping guide him up the stairs. He only took two steps before the flash backs of his fall, on the same set of stairs, whizzed through his mind.

"Matt, Matt… Matt?" A calming hand was placed on his shoulder.

"Are you ok? You were fitting around in your sleep."

It was Helen, and Matt was still sat in front of the TV with his dinner on his lap and the beer in his hand. Only he was dripping in sweat and sticking to the leather couch.

"I must have fallen asleep. Long day at my brothers with all that grafting."

"Well, what about this blood on your neck? Come to think about it, I cleaned a blood-stained shirt earlier today too."

"I didn't want to say. I was embarrassed. I think I cut myself when I fell down the stairs this morning. The gash must have reopened."

"It looks like an old wound."

Matt looked down at his shirt and it displayed a spreading pool of blood, so he rolled up the collar of the shirt to try and hide it.

"Hmm, weird," Matt looked puzzled.

The cut in the neck and shoulder region was healed, virtually scabbed over but the blood looked fresh.

"I don't know, I need shower," Matt finished up his meal and gulped a mouthful of booze before slumping back down into the couch. His legs were a bit unsteady.

Helen sat next to him to show comfort, the TV was also displaying her favourite reality show, so it was perfect. A two birds and one stone moment for her.

The physical body of Matt was a wreck, but his mind felt like it was in the early stages of a marathon. An hour of non sensical television seemed to give him ample time to drift off and rest. Hours passed without a flinch from Helen who had also passed out whilst snuggled up.

A mobile phone buzzed on top of the rustic living room table creating a loud enough vibration to wake the pair up. Groggy and fatigued, Matt held Helen up and propped her over his shoulder. He flicked off the TV in an unorthodox approach by pressing the standby button on the remote with his big toe.

She giggled like a young girl as they made their way upstairs. After a decade together, the spark was still there. There was minimal muscle mass within Matt's body, but Helens' petite and sleight body wasn't exactly taxing. Matt threw her doll like body down onto the bed. The fresh sheets provided a waft of lavender as she sunk down into the pleated duvet.

"I wish we did more together," Helen whispered.

That was a sure shot to ruin the mood and remove any lingering mojo from the room. Helen didn't elaborate any further, so Matt took the opportunity to head to the bathroom for a quick shower.

Matt looked baffled as he entered back into the bedroom. Helen had managed to get changed and fall asleep again in the space of his three-minute shower. The sound of dripping of water could be heard in the background. He searched the room for a knocked over glass but discovered it was himself, still soaked from the shower. Now he was grateful Helen was asleep, she would be furious with the amount of water he had dragged about.

He often muttered to himself in times of despair, "It's like I've bloody brought the bath in here. Anyway, since when does a carpet make for dripping sounds."

The bedside light was left on as he clambered into bed. It didn't deter him from falling asleep and he was out for the count as soon as his head hit the pillow.

CHAPTER 4

The breaks between branches of woodland trees revealed a silhouette of a male figure. Translucent cloud cover graced in front of a full moon provided convenient lighting for the dimly lit early morning.

"Who is this guy? Looks a bit weird."

"Just another walker, like us," a husky male voice replied.

A brisk post-winter nip in the wind forced the cuddling pair to pull up their coats and notch down their bobble hats. They seemed smitten with each other as their muddy boots squelched through the sludge and fallen twigs. Alice Hills was a bustling hotspot for dog walkers and ramblers, and nothing quite beats open fresh air in the morning. Even if it was bitterly cold and dark. It was spring after all and Christmas had only just been.

The topic of conversation was about the recent Christmas period. The pair of lovers were contemplating on what to do with each other for the next one.

"Where are we having dinner this year?" She asked.

Before he could respond, an ear shrieking sound of bird's squawks stopped them in their tracks. There must have been at least thirty birds smashing their way through the battered birch trees and ferns. The lack of leaves made it easy on the eye as the twosome awed above and followed the birds intended route up and out of the woods.

"Ravens!" He shouted.

He stumbled and tripped over a large fallen tree as he peered back over his shoulder. Landing in a puddle of mud, his body looked lifeless. His face was square down into the ground, the green coat he was wearing shrouded his head and shoulders.

"What are you doing? Get up."

She bent down onto her knees to turn his body over. The atmosphere had drastically changed. The ravens were no more, and the wind had died down. She pressed her gloved hand against the back of his head, but she screamed as his head twisted around.

His eyes had rolled back into his head as blood rushed to front of his skull. She pulled his hat off and it was evident that it was acting as a sponge for the gaping wound.

She cried in a panic as she shouted for help. Many thoughts rushed through her mind, *'how? He fell forward, why?'*. What seemed like a lifetime turned out to be about ten seconds as she lifted herself up. In the process of standing up she turned around on a pivot to look for help.

A man stood in front her, no more than five metres away. The unknown figure was male, standing taller than the smaller framed woman in front of him. He had broad shoulders and clutched a wooden baseball with two black stripes. The hood of his coat was up but the baseball style hat was unique. A two striped logo with a letter J adorned the front.

The female froze in her steps, she couldn't muster up any words. Murmurs from her dry lips along with trembling knees were a welcome sight for the attacker. He glanced over her shoulder to check that her lover was still down and out. He was. She tried to follow suit and look as well, but it was too late. The baseball bat raised high and firm. The head turn of the scared female was simultaneously met with a forceful swipe of the baseball that crashed into the forefront of her skull.

"Matt, Matt... Matt!"

"Where am I?"

"You've been sleep walking up and down the stairs for the last five minutes," Helen tried to explain but Matt looked exhausted.

"It's six o'clock, time to get up anyway. You're sweaty again, jump in the shower," she added.

His sleep walking was nothing new. He had done this so many times that Helen didn't think twice about waking him up and left him alone. Despite the history of his sleep walking Matt knew this episode was different. To dream about the same thing was rare. He appreciated that there were slight differences but he knew it was the same event.

'Should I tell Helen?', Matt thought deeply about his new dream and acknowledged how farcical his story was becoming.

Matt clambered out of the shower and dabbed himself dry. He flicked the light on, and an image of the attacker flashed within the large mirror on the wall in the hallway. He stepped back, aghast to what he had seen. It was too quick to take in any noteworthy details, but he knew it was the attacker. He spent the next thirty minutes getting dressed and making notes for his so-called investigation. He felt that the two dreams had too much in common with the recent woodland beating. He couldn't disregard it and set upon trying to piece things together.

"You ok up there?" Helen peered around the bannister. "I've made you some breakfast and a brew."

Matt was in the zone, pen in hand and perched on the end of the double bed with an A5 notepad filled with hypothetical scenarios. Breakfast was getting cold and so were his hunches, so he headed down the stairs. In his shirt and tie, work awaited. A much different day to the one before at his brother's house.

"I dreamed about the attack again," Matt blurted it out, he couldn't keep his thoughts to himself.

Helen didn't reply. Butter dripped from the toast onto Matt's tie as he waited for a response.

"Only this time, I know a bit more."

"Go on then," Helen's eyebrow raising was a sure sign of disbelief. She felt she was encouraging the madness rather than believing him.

"Well, I can't really remember the dialogue but look I've written down some notes."

Helen wasn't interested in reading about it and pushed the notepad into his chest. Matt took this as a sign of defiance, and he wanted to rebel.

"Well, the attacker was male. Not that I can remember what he looked like. You know in dreams that it's all a bit wishy-washy, the scenery seemed a bit different, but it was definitely Alice Hills. One hundred per cent," he paused and cut to the chase as Helen's patience seemed to be wearing thin.

"Anyway, he was wearing baseball cap. It was one of those 'Jolly' hats. And he had a baseball bat with a couple black stripes through it... That was the weapon," he was excited.

"Look, I get it. But, it's only a dream. Just coincidental. It's been on the TV and in the news a lot, so I think you're just subconsciously absorbing details of the real crime. Or should I say consciously?" Helen quipped back and pressed him towards the front door. A kiss goodbye, for now.

He was getting late for work and Helen needed to get back to her home office. The J hats, or Jolly hats as they known to the layman, are the 'in' thing at the moment. Matt secretly knew that the hat was far too commonplace to narrow down to anybody specific. The local news channel on the car radio played on the commute to work but there was only a small mention of the incident in Alice Hills. They made appeals for witnesses which never bodes well with a police investigation – a sign that they had no leads.

A quick kiss goodbye and I'm work bound in the car, back to reality, he thought. It was a good forty-five minute to his work but he was passing the crime scene on the way which was exciting for him. He was a city worker at a national car show room. Car show rooms need a decent population of people if they are to sell. Alice Hills was rural, and the site of cars were a bit of an ongoing issue with the local residents so a car show room wouldn't go down too well. Plenty of council applications had be vetoed against and ultimately disregarded.

The brow of the hill opened up the landscape and it showed a large police presence near the woods. His drive to work was usually numb and void, driving on auto pilot into the city was usually a guarantee bore fest but today was different.

The weaving country road was wet, slowly drying in the bright morning sun. The steady drive gave an opportunity to nosy in on the police entourage outside the gates of the crime scene. Matt couldn't help but notice a crowd forming. This was just the general public. They were an angry mob, more so than usual. If Alice Hills was known for anything within the county, then it was their busy body residents. Life was a constant battle with public outrage, and demonstrations were on a weekly agenda. If it wasn't Ethel sending leaflets through people's doors about poor car parking, then it was Gordon posting awkward social media messages relating to dog shit being rife on public footpaths.

A closer inspection revealed the white suits of a forensic crime team who were together with members of the media amongst a pool of police vehicles. Ethel would not be best pleased with the parking. The sight of all of this gave Matt some real detail to play alongside his vivid dreams.

Matt noticed two males in the crowd with 'J' hats on. He shook his head in disappointment but the other voices in his head refocussed him. *'The hat is common. A great way to confuse the police investigators,'* he thought to himself. Turning up to the crime scene in the same gear would be ballsy but a great reverse psychology trick.

The new detail from the recent dream at least narrowed down potential suspects. At least fifty per cent of the population anyway. The attacker was male. Not only that, but the orange boots, black hooded jacket and zipped waterproof trousers were unique. Maybe not individually but, as an ensemble they were. The 'J' hat only narrowed it further.

Then there was the baseball bat. Pine coloured with two black stripes through it. A baseball fan perhaps? Or just an overprotective house-proud man? Matt glanced to his passenger seat where his note pad of ideas had been strewn open.

Call it a sixty-minute drive, the inevitable traffic hit as Matt got onto the motorway. Wishing the day away, he couldn't wait to get home and go back to sleep. It seemed an odd concept to get excited about sleep without being tired. The more that Matt thought about the crime and his dreams, the more he felt he was pivotal to the investigation. He acknowledged that this whole notion was obscene. Too crazy to mention the police, telling his close family was enough for the time being.

The stop-start traffic required some attention. The lady driving alongside Matt was a welcome distraction. Matt glanced over his right shoulder for a mere few seconds, just long enough for the recipient of the stare to get the feeling they were being gazed upon. The slender brunette was singing away to the local radio station. Not a care in the world, the murder investigation was not on the forefront of her mind anyway. Matt's peripheral vision was blinkered as his pupils refocused through the side window of the passing vocalist. The repeated pervy looks from Matt eventually got a response. A frown from the woman instantly converted to a face of shock as Matt collided with the car in front. She carried on driving, with the feeling that Karma had been activated.

"Matt, Matt, Matt. Wake up!"

A clouded figure was shaking Matt's shoulders and what felt like a damp kiss was planted on his forehead. The low impact rear end crash was hard enough to trigger the airbags in Matt's car. His vision was blurry from all the dust from the airbag, and shouts of his name were echoed by the repeated and angry sounding horns of the passing vehicles.

"Where am I? Where am I? Helen?" Matt spluttered and waved his hands through the cloud of airbag dust.

"It's me. Ade. Are you ok, mate?"

"Ade? Fuck. I've hit you!?" Matt replied.

Ade was a colleague of Matt's. A fortunate element of the unfortunate event. The damage to both vehicles was only moderate so once they had both gathered their composure, they headed to the hard shoulder.

"The boss is going to go mental; I was already going to be late. It seems we were both going to be late," Ade was fuming.

"Sorry Ade, I've been distracted lately."

"Again?" Ade insinuated.

Ade was a towering figure, an exaggerated six and a half foot teamed with broad shoulders. When he wasn't selling 4X4's, he was in the gym. The single life and good income provided a quality lifestyle and image for Ade. The free company car helped as well.

Ade circled his vehicle whilst in a huff. A crick of the knees broke through the sound of passing cars as he bent down to inspect the damage up close. Raising his designer sunglasses onto his balding head, he squinted to focus on the damage, or lack thereof.

"There's nothing there," Matt mumbled.

Matt could see Ade's reflection in the chrome bumper, and he wasn't impressed.

"Your car is like a tank. Look at mine, there's nothing left of the front of it," Matt added.

The rage on Ade's face quickly faded as he began to realise that he and his vehicle was better off. His 4x4 did its job and a quick check over at the work garage would probably conclude no damage. The same couldn't be said for Matt's measly estate vehicle. The bumper was hanging off with obvious crumples.

"Sorry, mate. I just saw red. Look, pop your bumper in my boot and I'll tail you to work," Ade popped his sunglasses back down onto his nose. "Anyway, are you ok?"

The shock of the accident was too much for Matt, a small nod of the head is all he could muster up. Ade opened the boot of this vehicle as Matt was pulling the remains of the bumper away from his car. The flow of the traffic had sped up which made for a panicked rush to put the bumper into the boot of Ade's car.

Matt settled behind his steering wheel, double checking each component before starting the engine. A glance to the car in front was met with a puzzled look from Ade in the rear view mirror of his 4x4. Matt didn't need lip reading lessons to know that he shouted towards him, *'fucking come on then'*.

"So much for calming down."

It was a hesitant start back onto the motorway, but they got back on track without any issues. The rest of the journey to work was a repetition of both of them looking at each other through the rear-view mirror of Matt's car.

The late arrival through the forecourt at work was met by an unimpressed boss in the foyer. Laurissa was the best salesperson for the company, nationwide. Her steely looks were somewhat approachable so despite her obvious anger at the pair of her employees being late, it was a welcome start. For Matt anyway.

She noticed the car damage, the welcoming anger turned to fury. Both vehicles headed over to the onsite garage as Laurissa began to march in her smoothly ironed pin stripe suit. Matt and Ade barely had time to open the doors of their vehicles.

"What time is this? And do you both care to explain the damage?"

Ade looked at Matt to try and prompt an explanation.

"Sorry Loz, my fault. Just a simple hit in the rear."

The mechanic's introduction and obtaining of the keys interrupted the awkwardness.

"Just get into work. You're lucky we have no customers; this would have been a shocking advertisement for selling cars."

The pair of them followed Laurissa towards the office as the mechanic looked at the vehicle damage in frustration. The silence continued but the atmosphere was much calmer. They expected a harsher wrath from their boss.

Laurissa had worked hard to become the general manager of the showroom and she didn't want two employees wrecking her image and the PR status of the company. Both Matt and Ade knew what to do, they respected Laurissa so a hard day of graft and big sales was the least she would expect.

A finger tap to a diamond clad watch from Ade as he looked Matt square in the eye was Ade's subtle way of saying 'game on'. Matt psyched himself up with a big breath of air-conditioned office air and headed towards the cluster of customers waiting at the door.

Working hard wasn't exactly Matt's style. His job was a means to an end but today was different. Both his and Ade's reputation was on the line. There was no time to think about anything else but car sales. He knew that Ade would find this a doddle. Ade's physique was intimidating, he basically bullied customers into buying cars. Although his flirty style talking helped too.

"Rough day, boys?", Laurissa laughed.

They both knew that Matt's mistake worked into her hands. It was the end of the day and she got twice as much work out of the lads.

"Look, well done for today. Just be careful with the cars."

Matt and Ade were too exhausted to reply.

"Ade, you will need to drop Matt off at home. His car won't be repaired until tomorrow," she added.

"Can you not just lend him another…"

"Another car? No chance," Laurissa interrupted.

She turned and strutted away. Mission complete.

"You owe me a beer, come on. Close up, we're off to the pub," Ade pointed to the door.

Matt couldn't refuse after the trouble he had caused. He asked Ade for him to wait in the car so he could text Helen that he was going to be late back home. He typed what had happened but deleted it before he sent it. He was becoming more conscious to the madness he was creating and decided that Helen didn't need to know about the car accident. Matt had his own way of closing the workshop. His OCD in full effect – he checked all cupboards and cabinets were locked. Then double checked the toilets to ensure nobody was locked in before double tapping each door on the way out.

Eight hours had passed since the accident and whiplash was beginning to set in. A deep ache in his neck was adding to the reoccurring headaches. Locking the doors triggered a strain in his shoulder which was met with a coinciding heavy rainfall. *'Why?'* He cursed to himself as he pulled his jacket over his head and hopped around the puddles towards Ade's car.

Ade was chuckling to himself as the creak of the passenger door opened. The large 4x4 required a big step up into the seat which caused more laughter from Ade as Matt struggled and writhed in pain. The click of the seat belt and shake of the wet jacket resulted in a sigh of relief from Matt. He could only laugh back and was happy for the relaxed positive vibe that Ade was giving off.

The muscle-bound dark physique of Ade filled out the interior of the car. The same couldn't be said for Matt. Small talk and quick apologies from the pair of them filled in the time as they made their way to the pub.

A stretch of the arms and neck from Matt led to him seeing a 'J' hat on the back seat. It had seen better days and had plenty of use. He knew that Ade didn't live in his neck of the woods and this had Matt thinking, *why was he driving from the direction of where I live? How often does he do that?* The shock of the accident meant he had not thought of this earlier on.

Matt glanced back and forth to the hat and Ade. Trying to piece together more of the puzzle and put Ade into the detail of attack. Fortunately for Matt, Ade was fixated to the road. The accident had caused him to concentrate more on the road.

Ade certainly has the physical presence of this attacker. Matt was still certain that his dreams were relevant to the attack. *Ade? Surely not,* Matt thought to himself. They had worked together for years and Matt felt he knew him inside out. Matt gazed out of the window trying to focus on the inner detail of his dreams. He couldn't remember what the attacker looked like, only that he was male. Ade is built like a body builder with a dark complexion, but Matt couldn'tt recollect a simple detail like the colour of the attackers skin.

"Oi, Matt!", Ade shouted as he shut the door. "We're here."

They had already arrived at the pub and Matt was fixated on a lamp post at the rear of the car park. Ade waddled towardsthe door of the pub; his legs barely able to carry his triangle shaped upper frame.

Matt took his time to walk through the dimly lit car park as he saw Ade ordering some beers at the bar. It was pitch black. He was kicking up the stones within the car park and walking in circles trying to muster up some courage. The tempo of the strides increased, partly due to how cold it was, but more so to ignite ideas on how to question Ade. Ade had suddenly become suspect number one in Matt's rash thinking mind.

Heading through door of the pub instantly cleared Matt's mind on what was he was supposed to ask. He was a bumbling wreck; he was about to interrogate a good work friend about a murder. All based on a 'J' hat that a million and one people own. Matt smirked at the absurdity of all.

"Am I ok getting a double?" Matt quivered.

"I've got you a beer now", Ade passed him an ice-cold pint. "Are you ok? You're shaking."

"Yea, just cold out there. Brrr," Matt shook his body as though he had just entered the room from a blizzard.

"Grab a seat, I'll just a get a whiskey to warm the cockles," Matt pointed to an empty table.

Ade took a sip of his beer as he trudged along the sticky patterned carpet. His face was void of any emotion, the clumsy explanation of being cold from Matt seemed to have worked but it hadn't boosted any further encouragement to ask questions.

Matt had already downed his double whiskey and was well into his pint of beer by the time he took his seat.

"One day of graft leads you to this? You look a broken man," Ade quipped.

"Yea, pretty much," Matt shaked.

Question calling from the quiz master in the background provided an echo chamber for the pair to talk. Matt looked at the quizzer in awe trying to absorb some of the confident public speaking. Flitting his eyes back and forth, tapping his feet and flipping beer mats up and down, Matt was the polar opposite. The atmosphere was awkward, and Ade was staring Matt down noticing that he couldn't sit still.

"Look, can we forget about today? The cars are getting fixed, we've still got our jobs and we're both alive to tell the story," Ade broke the ice.

Matt stopped the fidgeting with a wry smile. He glanced over both shoulders, making sure nobody was watching. Leaning forward with a short cough, Matt was preparing his first question.

"It could be worse, we could be like that couple up in Alice Hills," Ade added and acknowledged Matt's smile as agreement to his earlier question.

Matt took another look around with a gulp of his beer. Ade had instigated the conversation of the crime which was job number one for Matt.

"Yea, what do you think about that?" Matt asked.

Ade shrugged. This got Matt's thoughts in overdrive. Would a perpetrator really be so confident in bringing the subject up?

"Maybe this is some reverse psychology shit?"

"What is?" Ade replied.

"Sorry, I was thinking out aloud. Another beer?" Matt redirected the conversation.

Ade tilted his glass, enough had been drank to warrant another beer so he gave the nod. Matt necked back another double whiskey at the bar before ordering more beers and yet another whiskey.

Neither of them had ever been big drinkers and Matt knew this. He was aware of the consequences of drinking whiskey. The crime had become his focal point and a bit of Dutch courage was needed in order to ask Ade some questions. Matt was constantly double checking his line of thought. *What would be the chances of the attacker being the first person I ask questions to? Especially somebody I knew* – Matt continually questioned his own motives.

"So, they reckon the attacker was wearing a 'J' hat," Matt mumbled with a packet of pork scratchings in his mouth.

Ade traced Matt's eyeline to the nearby local newspaper, "They did? I don't know much about it to be honest."

A rush of blood shot to his Matt's head and lit his face up like up a red traffic light. He suddenly remembered that the hat was within his dream and not in the news. Only he knew about this potential aspect of the crime.

"You have the same hat and you was also coming back from Alice Hills this morning," Matt blurted it out.

He clearly wasn't cut out for this detective business.

"You wouldn't make a good police officer, mate", Ade laughed. "Are you seriously implying that I had something to do with that attack?"

Ade was shocked. He didn't know whether to laugh or cry as he gave stern eye contact.

"You're being serious aren't you?" Ade leant forward.

"No, no no. Sorry, I've just had a lot on," Matt tried to calm Ade down.

"Let's try this day again. I'm not having a simple car accident wreck our relationship," Ade reverted back to the crash again.

Ade was happy to negotiate a fresh start despite the lateness of the day. Matt held out his hand and was grateful for Ade's understanding. Not that Ade understood Matt's predicament, he presumed the whole meltdown was because of the morning car accident.

Each double whiskey was going down a little too well for Matt's liking but he seemed to be relaxing and forgetting about work and the crime. The physical effects of the Whiskey helped too, as it took the edge off the neck pain.

What should have been a quick beer after work turned into a heavy session. For Matt anyway. Ade finished the night with a few glasses of water to drown out the early beers in preparation for the drive home.

The ring of the bell for the last orders had rang at least five minutes after their last purchase and the pair of lads were outstaying their welcome. The bar manager loitered near their table and collected the near empty glasses signalling them to leave.

The car park was covered in a thin layer of ice that glistened under the moonlight. Ade acted as a walking aide for Matt and propped him up on the way to the car.

"Who is that?" Matt pointed a wearily finger towards a dark figure on the opposite side of the car park.

"I don't know. Look, lets just get to the car and home," Ade didn't even look over. He just wanted to hurry up and get home.

"I see him now. It's a child," Matt uttered as the unknown person stepped out from the darkness and under a streetlight.

"There is nothing there," Ade replied. He had succumbed to Matt's persistence and curiosity got the better of him.

"Yes, it's a boy dressed in eighties clothing," Matt focussed his eyes for a moment. "He looks just like me."

"You're drunk, come on," Ade started to man handle Matt and used his physique to control the situation. "You're an adult, not a child. And you're here with me so how can you be there."

"No, no, no. It's me as a child. The hair, the looks, the clothes. It's all me." Matt slurred and slipped on the ice banging his head in the process.

"Matt, are you ok?" Ade sat Matt up.

"Yea, yea," Matt stood himself and brushed himself off.

The alcohol had subsided in a matter of seconds. The panic of the slip had partly sobered him up, and he looked over to where he had seen the boy but there was nothing there. Matt's mind was all over the place, he was certain that he had seen his younger self but persuaded himself to forget about it and blame it on the booze.

"Thanks buddy," Matt slurred as Ade fastened his seat belt.

"There we go, all set. Let's get you home."

Ade cautiously reversed from the car park as Matt slumped across to reach into the rear seat.

"What you doing, stop messing about, Matt."

Matt turned around; glass eyed with his mouth gawped open. He had put on the J hat.

"Not funny, mate. Put it back."

A quick, limp, drunken toss of the hat from Matt sobered him up slightly. He knew he had gone a step too far. Matt took out his mobile phone and noticed he had several missed calls and messages. All from Helen - *'Where are you?'* "*Are you ok?'*. Panic set as he realised that he had forgot to tell Helen what he was doing. *'She's probably thinking I've gone and done something stupid'*, Matt thought to himself. The last text message brought some relief as she confirmed that his boss, Laurissa, had told Helen of their whereabouts.

"I'm sorry for today. I've been having weird dreams," Matt straightened up as Ade focussed on the road. "It's these dreams, they've been about..."

"We'll get you home. Rest up and I'll see you tomorrow," Ade interrupted. "Not that I need to explain myself, but I think it'll help you sleep better and stop looking at me as the attacker. I've been seeing a girl from the gym over in Alice Hills and I stay over every now and again."

Ade had plenty of conquests from his gym. This is what he called them, conquests. His broad macho image carried every stereotypical trait you could think of. Matt nodded to Ade to acknowledge his admission but deep inside he felt stupid. The last day had been a whirl wind and he had been caught up in his own façade. Accusing a good friend of such a heinous crime was a new low for Matt and the embarrassment was setting in and clear to see on Matt's face.

"And the J hat… Well you know me; I fall for every fashion faux pas going," Ade added.

Matt laughed and gave a play jab to Ade's muscly arm. The men rarely talked to each other, and small interactions like this represented a million words. All was well in the world and this chapter could now be closed. There was no need for sloppy apologies. Ade had a reputation to uphold.

Driving this late at night provided quiet roads, the noise pollution of the City muzzled into the distance as they got further away from the motorway. Lights were scarce on Matt's home street, but they were greeted by a bright light as they pulled up outside the house. It was the living room window and Helen was stood centrally with her arms folded, causing a big silhouette to shadow onto the bonnet of Ade's car.

"Déjà vu of Laurissa this morning," Ade laughed.

Matt grabbed a few mints from the dashboard and instantly sobered up at the thought of Helen shouting at him. Another jab to Ade's arm and he left the car towards the house. The growling sound of Ade's 4x4 echoed away as he left Matt to meet his fate. Matt tried to concentrate on walking straight but the more he did, the more he swayed.

The house key didn't even have chance to enter the grand double door. Helen gave the door a swift opening, "You're drunk".

There was no point in denying it. The mints were not enough to fool Helen. Helen was bemused, he was a regular drinker in his younger years and constantly made a fool of himself. This recent example only brought back bad memories, and in turn, frustration for Helen.

"You've just trawled through the flower beds, get in the shower," Helen pointed up the stairs. "Why do I always seem to be telling you to get into the shower?"

Matt turned to observe the trail of destruction that he caused. He believed he had walked quite well from the car. The flower beds were ruined but the beautiful fir tree to the side caused a good distraction from the devastation. Or so he would hope. Matt and Helen planted the fir tree when they first moved into the house. They wanted it would grow alongside their love and life.

Helen went straight to bed. She was clearly annoyed but the fact she stayed up to wait for her husband was a sign that she cared for him.

The next twenty minutes involved Matt showering and drinking copious amounts of water to try and sober up. He had work in the morning and didn't fancy having Helen and his boss, Laurissa, giving him grief. Just one of them would be enough to cope with, two would be hard to comprehend.

Matt slumped quietly into bed alongside Helen. At least she let him in. There have been times in the past where he has been summoned to the spare room. The fresh bedding still lingered a smell of Lavender which is why Helen was out for the count. Matt was happy to see her asleep, not for the beauty of her looks, but it was the only reason he was allowed in the bed.

CHAPTER 5

A whistle echoed through the tunnel of trees to reach out for man's best friend. A bark in response triggered a return to the owner.

"That dog has just splashed my leg," a female voice mumbled to her linked arm lover.

"Sorry, he's just excited to see you," the dog walker replied.

The male put his arm around the slightly smaller female he was out walking with. Their matching dark green jackets and black trousers was a usually a trait of young twins but, the kiss to the head through the bob hat from the male was confirmation that they were lovers.

"Can we talk about kids?" the male asked and the atmosphere drastically changed.

"You know how it is, can we talk about this another time?" An angered reply from the female.

It was clear that this type of conversation had occurred on more than one occasion. The male took the snappy response as a final answer and shuffled ahead to signal they needed to get a move on.

"These boots are crap," she pointed to a hole in the side. "We need some like this guy up there."

"Matching boots as well?" he laughed. "He seems a bit shady anyway, why would you want to look like that."

The frosty fog covered some considerable ground, but the approaching figure adorned a pair bright orange boots that lit up the area with every step. Like a boat approaching a coastline, the boots acted like a lighthouse the closer the loving pair approached the advancing male.

The female linked her partner closer; a sense of fear stretched across her face. A responding rub of her gloved hand from the male partner was a subtle gesture that everything was going to be fine.

"Morning," the male tried to acknowledge the approaching orange boot cladded character.

There was no reply, his head was embedded inside a black zipped hooded jacket. The zipped black trousers did raise initial suspicion, but the male comforted the female with a nod and smile. The arms of the pair relaxed a little as they both looked over their shoulder to see the passer by disperse into the fog.

A sudden rush of rainfall blistered through the trees. It was almost as if the tree cover no longer existed. The walking pair instantly looked like drowned rats, drenched head to toe. It was normal for the weather in this part of the country to be intermittent and random. There were never any warning signs for this. A pre check of the weather from the male confirmed it that was supposed to be dry and clear. They both glanced up with expressions of confusion, and distraught etched across their faces.

"Come on, we need to be quick. Let's see if those holey boots can hurdle logs. You first," the male pointed out to a fallen tree.

There were plenty of fallen trees in Alice Hills but this tree seemed to require a pole vault. The female went first, she felt she was setting the standard, but he was gauging whether it was physically possible. Slightly cheating by raising her left leg onto the log, she managed to spring herself over with a helping hand.

The splash of mud and water on the other side caused the female to curse as it seeped into the now much larger hole in her boot. He laughed as she struggled to her feet, sliding in each direction trying to stabilise herself. He stepped back, he questioned his own ability as a million and one thoughts rushed through his mind. *Can I do this? What if I hurt myself? I'm not thirteen years old anymore!*

The female could not bear to watch and covered her head with her muddied gloves. It wasn't noticeable earlier, but the birds were providing a tranquil ambience to the spring cold. Only now, they had stopped suddenly, and their sudden silence was obvious to them both.

A blistering home run strike of a baseball bat struck the back of the head of the male. Despite the mass of puddled mud throughout the woods, there was no sound of an approaching figure from behind. The slumping thud of a body was loud enough for the female to think her partner had made the jump. The squawking of ravens provided a background track as the fingers parted away from the female's face.

She rushed over to the body, her clothing now completely drenched and weighing her down. Lying flat and face down, he looked lifeless. Her feet slid back with each step forward, the mud was acting like a travellator. The run soon turned to a crawl as she got on both knees for better traction, desperate to get to the male body. There was no call of a name from her, just a mixed bundle of groans and emotion fuelled pleas that everything was going to be okay.

It only took a matter of seconds for the dirty gloves to be soaked in ruby red blood. There was nothing she could do; she had no medical skills. Not even basic CPR. If this wasn't the end, then the mounting levels of water would make sure of it.

"Why did you do it!" the attacker towered over the lifeless body. "You're next."

A beard. A faceless beard gaped through the zipped jacket adorned with a 'J' hat. She had enough time to recognise the orange boots and black trousers of the attacker. The earlier tension she embodied had now been justified but it was too late.

She gasped and begged for mercy to the faceless man. Wiping the mix of tears and rainwater from her face she could only rise to her knees with one last plea, "please, please." But, there was no hesitation. The bat swooped down and smashed into the females tear draped face.

"Matt, oh Matt," Helen whispered into a dreary Matt's ear.

Matt slapped her hand away as he pried his eyes open from a deep sleep.

"What are you doing? I'm piss wet through?" he barked.

Helen laughed as she continued to spray Matt with water from a small canister. A form of pay back as Matt had bought the sprayer as part of a cheap hairdresser kit one Valentine's Day.

"Hungover much?" Helen tried a rhetorical question.

"You'd think so but I'm fine. I don't know how. Those Whiskeys went down too easy. I don't even remember going to sleep," Matt replied. "Look, I know it's crazy but we need to talk about these dreams of mine."

Helen, out of sympathy, held his hand and acknowledged the request. She had previously joked about the situation, but she could sense the tone of fear and puzzlement in Matt's voice. His struggling mental characteristics were matched with physical symptoms too. He had slept naked, or at least stripped down at some point in the middle of the night – dripping in sweat. Whereas Helen had slept in an elegant pair of silk flowery pyjamas. Another Valentine's Day gift from Matt. The sweat stains on the adjacent cover sheets were obvious; what was light blue, was now nearing a black colour.

Helen made her way to the shower as Matt gathered his thoughts with a biro onto a nearby notepad. He jotted everything down from the recent dream within five minutes, knowing that minor details of a dream could quickly disperse. The pen and pad slammed onto the bed side table as though he had just finished a high school exam in the very last second.

He pushed his naked body up off the low rising bed and strutted to the bathroom. The blinds on the passing windows had already been opened by Helen but he didn't care. If anything, he slowed down in the hope some peering eyes would see. The newfound information from his dream had worked up his confidence and libido. Helen dripped out of the shower and proceeded to grab a towel from the rack just as Matt entered the room.

She glanced at his midriff and knew where this was heading, "No, you're sweaty and you stink of stale beer. Get in the shower."

Matt ignored her and proceeded to pull her against the wall. Helen embraced the rare intimacy. *A second shower wouldn't be so bad*, she thought.

Helen's left leg raised as her back pressed against the wall. Matt complied and held the leg in place with his right forearm, not quite strong enough to use the grip of his hand. Kissing each other's neck, Matt thrusted in sync with the dripping shower. She raised her hands and scrunched her wet hair, accentuating her deep brown eyes for Matt to focus on.

He loved her eyes. It was what had attracted him to her all those years ago. He cusped her right breast as he out sped the pace of the shower drip.

"OK, we need a shower," Helen pulled Matt away from the wall.

His sweat had exacerbated, and he breathed heavily entering the shower. Matt held up the shower gel and splashed a bit into his palm. He had barely put the shower gel back down as he found his hand pressed against Helen's breast again. Helen needed a second instalment, the earlier three minutes clearly not getting the job done.

It took a while to get restarted but they had both got the morning off to a good start. Matt was much quicker at getting ready than Helen, so he was frantically setting the dining room table. They never ate breakfast in a formal manner, but Matt had a spring in in his step and felt Helen was willing to listen the outrageous detail of his dreams.

Place mats were positioned across from each other alongside some silver cutlery. He placed his notepad beside his glass of orange juice. Footsteps echoed through the hallway, Helen was on her way. Matt anxiously adjusted the notepad, his focal point on the dining table.

"Need any help?" Helen asked as Matt was struggling to butter the toast and pour coffee.

"No, take a seat through there."

Helen peered through the glass door to the table. She was impressed and smiled back to a silent and focused Matt. Morning sex and cooked breakfast, today was good day. She headed through to the dining room, it was reasonably modern in comparison to the rest of the house. Helen designed the whole house to keep in line the age of the building, but Matt was allowed one room to express himself. He kept it flush white, plain and simple.

"Hey, hold on," Matt caught Helen flipping through his notepad as he placed down the bacon and toast on the table.

"Sorry but I am honestly intrigued now. Three nights of the same dream isn't chance," she sat up and pulled her chairs towards the table.

He flipped through the two pages of notes he had prepared to refresh his memory. He was excited, he wanted to blurt out all the details. The knobbly index finger of his right hand ran line by line through the notes to help compose himself. Gulping a mouthful of coffee, he coughed to clear his throat.

"I'm happy you're taking me serious."

"I always…"

"No, let me finish. I know that we haven't always seen eye to eye. Me wanting kids and you… well not wanting them."

"I do, times have changed. A female body can wait much longer these days. I just want my career to get to the next chapter," she held out her hand across the table. "That's all."

Matt lifted her hand and kissed the marriage ring. He had bought the glistening diamond encrusted ring as an intended engagement ring from a local pawn shop. Helen was happy with the ring but ended up picking her own engagement ring from a reputable jeweller. It was not uncommon for Helen to call the shots. Matt looked up into her brown eyes as memories of controlling situations flashed through his mind. She was always picking which restaurant they ate at and she also picked the car he drove (despite it being a company car and him being a car salesman). The mounting small incidents were building to a much larger problem so this talk about his dream seemed like a change in a positive direction.

"I promise we'll try for kids soon. Anyway, come on. Let's get started on the details of this dream."

They both gulped more coffee as their hands parted ways. An air of pressure was lifted, and a positive ambience was left lingering.

Matt rustled up his note pad and banged it on the table imitating a news reader.

"Right. I've had three dreams and the focal point has always been the same," Matt held out three fingers with an emphasis on the index finger as he said the word same.

"The attack?"

"Yea, its' always involved a male attacker against this loving couple walking through Alice Hills. Only that some of the little aspects have differed in each one."

"Like what?" Helen was acting like she was working. A lawyer's instinct was to question, constantly.

"It's hard to explain but it's the little things. This morning for example. You woke me up by spraying water in my face. Well, that somehow triggered heavy rainfall in my dream. Only, it had never rained in the previous dreams. And the way the woman reacts to her partner when he gets hit. It just wasn't the same as before."

Dreams would often be logical at the time of having them. Matt used to have a reoccurring dream where he drove a car without wheels. It was something he would laugh about as he managed to get out and about driving it. It all made sense whilst he was dreaming, no questions asked. The nonsensical nature of it would only be apparent the next day when he was awake.

"Dreams are inspired from your own thoughts so maybe that's why you're trying to link it somebody you know," Helen tried to put some logic to the dream.

"Possibly. Some of the conversations are slightly different too."

"I think we would know by now if the victims or attacker was somebody we knew — we have a small circle of friends and family."

She seemed to make a bit of jump on the topic. Matt shook his head a little, but he knew she was right. He needed to look further afield. Cringe and embarrassment filtered through his body as he thought about yesterday. Blaming a work friend for a crime that only he knew about through his dreams was ridiculous.

"I can't explain any of this but why have I dreamed three nights in a row about a real-life crime. Not only that, but I know some intricate details of the same attack."

"But not all of the details. Not yet anyway, the police or media haven't gone into that much depth," Helen gave a lifeline of hope for Matt. "Come on then, what else do you know from the dream last night? What else do you know that hasn't been released by the police yet?"

Matt placed his head in his hands to recollect images. He glanced through the notepad one more time.

"Well, all of the dreams have kind of blurred into one so I'm just going to throw everything at you. The victims…"

The sudden realisation across both of their face lit up the room. *Why had his focus always been on the attacker?*

"You haven't really mentioned them before. It was always the attacker, if you narrow that down then maybe you can find somebody with a motive," Helen said pragmatically.

"Good idea," It seemed obvious now that somebody else pointed out. "The woman is definitely a slightly smaller frame than the man and they were both wearing an identical dark green jacket with black trousers. Matching black hats and gloves... The woman had a hole in her boot."

"What? Matching clothes? What are they, twins?" Helen laughed. "What about their faces?"

"All faces were blurred. There was even a dog walker with a blurred face. The only distinction I can remember about any face was with the attacker. He had a beard. Just a head with a J hat on and a beard."

"Where are you in this dream? The dreams that I have, always have me as myself and involved with the story. Like a main character," Helen asked.

"I'm there, nobody can see me though. It's like I'm following along as a camera man," Matt was trying to animate how it works. "Dreams are weird."

Helen started making her own notes on Matt's notepad. Matt could see a bullet point list alongside headings of the people involved in his dream. MALE ATTACKER; MALE AND FEMALE VICTIMS – BASEBALL BAT ATTACK TO THE SKULLS OF THE VICTIMS.

"OK, from what I remember, you have told me the following," Helen pointed to further text on her notepad. Legs crossed and really invested.

Matt peered over. To his surprise she had been listening and acknowledging detail of his previous dreams too.

"You said yesterday and the day before that the attacker had black zipped trousers and orange boots. We also know that they are male with a beard. He also wore a black hooded jacket that was zipped up," she ticked each point in sequence.

"And a 'J' hat. Baseball cap," Matt added.

"Anything else?" The expression on Helen's face said it all as she looked perplexed. This was nothing to go off.

"Well, the striped baseball bat and I heard him talk as well."

Helen was shocked that this had not been mentioned earlier, "What did he sound like? What did he say?"

"The tone and sound of his voice isn't obvious. Thinking about it, I can't think of any distinction in any of the voices within the dream. I think that's just a weird dream thing."

"Makes sense… Come on then. What did he say?" Helen seemed unconvinced but proceeded anyway.

"He said, *Why did you do it* and *you're next*, to the woman after he had attacked the man."

"I remember the couple talking about kids too. But, I remember the male arguing for kids in one dream and then vice versa in the other dream," Matt added in a blasé fashion.

"What? Like us? Just the bit about kids, I mean. I think your real-life experiences are creating this. There is too much coincidence. Especially with you blaming Ade as well yesterday," Helen lifted her arms aside. "I can't believe I'm going to say this. I sort of believe that you're onto something, but you need to work what is reality and what is from your memory."

Matt had completely forgotten about the Ade situation for a moment. He looked embarrassed, not only because he blamed a good friend for an attack that he had spun his own hypothesis on but, because he was drunk. Separating realism from deep rooted memories seemed impossible. Matt knew this was a big task. He was still having doubts – *can somebody really dream about a crime and find the attacker?*

"Maybe the drink last night has messed me about a bit."

Helen finished up her notes and passed the notepad back over to Matt with a nod in agreement. She got up out of her seat, brushed the toast crumbs off her lap and made her way to the home office.

"Yea, you're right," Matt shouted.

Helen turned back around to see what he was referring to.

"I need to go to the scene of the crime and see if I can build a better picture of the area. Maybe it'll help for my next dream."

"Well, I didn't mean it like it that, but I suppose it won't do any harm."

Matt sensed a turn in the conversation and didn't want it to worsen. The conversation and relationship had gone well until the end. He pulled out his phone and brought up Laurissa in his contacts. Before dialling he caught the eye of Helen again.

"Am I going to dream about this every day? Until it's solved?" he expected Helen to have an answer. "I can't do this, I basically accused Ade of it just because he had the same hat. I need to visit the crime scene."

Helen closed the office door, but she could still see Matt through the glass window as he raised his mobile phone to his ear. She watched him as he leant against the wall pressing the light switch by accident. He nervously flicked it off again as the recipient answered the phone. Helen couldn't believe it; he was ringing in sick for a few days. The single glass paned door wasn't soundproof, but Helen opened the door to make sure that she was hearing it right.

Disgust was evident in both her face and stance as she stood in the doorway with her hand on her hip and reading glasses atop of her head.

"What?" Matt shrugged his shoulder.

"You're a good liar."

Helen had good instincts when it came to seeking truths. It was this particular trait that led her on the career path of a Lawyer. She would often boast that it was her sixth sense. From playing games like Two Truths and a Lie in the school playground, to helping her friends and family catch out dubious characters and questionable partners – she had an underlying psychological skill.

"I'm not lying. I'm still in pain. My neck is killing me from the accident. It seems worse today."

"But you're going to the crime scene acting like Sherlock Holmes?"

"I need this, Helen," Matt fretted as he searched for Helen's car keys.

Helen tossed her keys from the side cabinet; Matt's car was still in the works garage. He caught the array of key rings at a stretch and mocked Helen's throwing technique. She was a career professional, but the playful key rings she had showed she had an immature and down to earth side.

The roar of the engine reverberated off the driveway as he reversed away. It was still early in the morning and if the neighbours weren't awake, they would be now. It was eight thirty as he glanced at the digital clock on the dashboard. He double checked the time against his watch and noticed it was broken. The watch was stuck at seven thirty AM. A shake of the arm had no effect at restarting it. It was a gift from Helen, much better than the presents he bought her so he knew that a repair was a must.

Matt wasn't a petrol head, but he enjoyed driving Helen's car. It was another company car through his firm – they provided an allowance which could be split within the family if required. His colleague, Ade, used the whole allowance on a huge 4x4. Matt however, had to opt for a smaller car so the rest of his allowance could be used for Helen's car. She argued that she needed a good-looking car for work to keep up appearances.

The eyes of morning joggers and dog walkers observed the black Mercedes in awe, as it passed. It had element of pretentiousness. It was a real ego booster that gave Helen confidence before entering a court room. It was also supporting Matt towards the crime scene.

Matt avoided the rural country roads and stuck to major roads, the mishap with the truck had caused more worry than the later accident on the motorway with Ade. The car had a voice recognition system, so Matt used it to turn on the local news channel. He was hoping for an update on the case before going to the crime scene.

Heading to the motorway resulted in a dead end due to roadworks so reluctantly, he carried on through to a different A road. The brown coloured tourist roadside sign at the next set of traffic lights confirmed Alice Hills car park was ten miles away.

The detour provided ample time for Matt to get his head straight. He was certain that he knew the attacker and both victims – *would this visit trigger anything else?* He felt a purpose in life for the first time in a long time. He did not dislike his job; he just didn't love it. He wanted Helen's passion for her job in something he could do.

The news channel was all politics for the next twenty minutes, but the local bulletins were due to start as he pulled into Alice Hills carpark. The police presence was still clear to see but they hadn't blocked off the car park. He reversed, using the rear view camera to guide the car into a parking bay outlined by gravel when the intro for the news bulletin started. It was short lived as his mobile started to ring through the media system and interrupt the news reader.

"Brother, are you and Helen still up for the meal at ours later on?" Josh had interrupted the news bulletin.

"Yea, we'll be there."

"Good… Look, Helen called Amy and she's worried about you."

Matt clenched his fists; he needed to listen to the radio, but he couldn't cut his brother off. The call was concern for his wellbeing and Matt couldn't dismiss it. Cutting him off would only amplify the situation.

"I'm ok. I just need some time to relax. You know, get away from work and all that," Matt said in a calm manner.

"I know you've gone up to Alice Hills to solve, this dream, slash, crime of yours."

"Fuck, why has she told you that?" Matt didn't keep his calm for long.

"We're all worried about you. Look, do not do anything daft and we'll see you tonight."

The news reader had finished an article on a national scandal about Z list celebrities just as Josh hung up the phone.

"We have an update in relation to the gruesome attack in local Alice Hills."

Matt took his seat belt off and pulled the lever under his seat to slide it back. A glare from the police officer across the car park operating the gate into the woods was one of either concern or curiosity. Matt couldn't tell but he wasn't having somebody else disrupt him. The rest of the car park was empty, and it should have been common sense that this side of the woods would be closed off.

"The police have confirmed that the middle-aged male victim is in a stable condition. An urgent TV appeal is due to air on national news tonight, but they are asking for any potential witnesses to contact them as soon as possible. We wish the victim and his family all the best and we hope they pull through."

The bulletin was very succinct considering the severity of the crime. Matt's anxiety and heart rate was rising. He could feel the heartbeat pounding through his chest and he clutched the same. A shooting pain drove across his chest and through to his arm before ending in a pinching feeling towards his wrist. The blood flow and reaction to the news was something he had never experienced before.

Knock, knock.

A truncheon tapped on the tinted driver side window. His vehicle was less than subtle, even more so in a vacant car park next to the crime scene. Matt used the electric window and pulled himself up from his slump. He lifted the sleeve of his shirt and swiped it across his forehead to wipe the sweat away. There was no hiding his perspiration though. The knock at the window was a welcome distraction and within seconds Matt was composed and alert. The chest pain not only subsided but completely disappeared.

"Are you ok sir?" the female officer addressed Matt.

The key was still in the ignition with the radio playing. Matt turned and pulled the key out to silence the car.

"Yes, ma'am," Matt caught the collar number and name of the officer as he gave eye contact. Phillips 7845. "Sorry, I came up here for some fresh air and forgot all about the incident. Such a travesty."

"Yes. It is still under investigation. The victim is our priority."

"Well, can I get in over that way?" Matt pointed to the other side. "Hang on, Victim? Not plural?"

"The other side is fine sir."

Officer Phillips walked away abruptly. She had barely said ten words, but it was enough to potentially prejudice the case. Her hope of questioning him further quickly deteriorated.

Matt took the lack of confidence from the rookie officer as an opportunity to quickly make his way to the other side of the woods. He felt guilty, the look of embarrassment across her face before she left was plain to see. A police officer placed at the scene of the biggest crime of Alice Hills' history should probably have acted with more diligence. Or at least have had a supporting officer. The lack of high-profile crimes in this area had limited the experience of not only police officers but, the police force in general. The police officers of Alice Hills were usually giving out litter and speeding fines, a far cry away from grievous bodily harm cases and murder attempts.

A calm wind softened the quiet atmosphere. The silence was broken every so often by a beep on the stranded police officer's radio. Matt knew being up here was risky, he was fortunate that it was a novice police officer who greeted him. Anybody with a bit of nous about them would have sent Matt back home. He checked back as he passed through the gate and into the dense conifer lined walkway – the coast was clear.

Matt loved this area of Alice Hills, the back-gate entrance loops around to the vicinity of the attack. *Where is the police presence?* It was deserted. The images of the dream flashed through his head as he tried to visualise the exact location of the attack. He was certain he knew where it happened, the storm a few years back caused havoc and dropped a selection of large trees on this side of Alice Hills. The hurdling actions of the male and female victims by the dead tree was around here somewhere and Matt knew it.

Matt and Josh were regular visitors to the woods as youngsters. Riding their bikes through the rough terrain provided plenty of fun and mishaps. The blueprint of the whole area was mapped inside of his head – he knew the layout like the back of his hand. If anybody could avoid police attention, then it was Matt. Flashbacks ran through his mind as he looked in each direction. The tree to his left used to have a rope swing hanging from it and a friend of Josh broke his collarbone when he fell from it. The mounds to the right-hand side provided the perfect circuit for their mountain bikes, again, one of Josh's friends broke a bone in the process of playing on them.

Matt's reminiscences transitioned to reality as he faded further into a daydream. His visions came to life as he saw his younger self and brother right in front his eyes. Matt looked around, the police were still visible, but they did not see the kids playing on the swing rope screaming and shouting at one another. A younger Matt flew off the swing from a great height and landed in a fresh puddle of squelching mud. Matt stared, flummoxed at the sight of himself as a child. This particular day was just like any other day, playing outside and enjoying life, but the act of seeing it unfold in front of him brought out the exact moment out from his memory bank. Younger Matt brushed down his filthy denim dungarees, a sign of the times. The t-shirt underneath the dungaree's was of an image of an old video game further confirming Matt's thoughts that it was him as a child.

That t-shirt was thrown away after this day as it was too dirty. Ruined, he thought to himself. Matt locked eyes with his younger self as they stared at each other. *Can he see me?* he thought. Youthful Josh shouted to young Matt asking if he was ok, but the pair of Matts continued to stare at each other.

"Sorry, I thought I saw somebody," young Matt replied.

Matt didn't have chance to recall further on the vivid flashback as his memories were randomly interrupted by thoughts of Helen's earlier theory; *Are my dreams a jigsaw and my memories the pieces? Am I building a story that just so happens to be a coincidence of the crime?*

He winced as he clambered over a stile, catching his groin area on a loose piece of barbed wire. Being quiet was pivotal if he was to get any closer the scene – although he still didn't know what he was looking for. His teeth gritted and he gasped further as the razor-sharp blade of the barbed wire pulled from his trousers. Leaving a trail of blood behind.

The crunch of the dry twigs that had fallen from the leafless trees of the recent winter didn't help Matt's cause either. He pulled his jeans up and crouched down. He was right about the crime location; glancing through the trees he could see three, four… five police officers surrounding a cordoned off area, all stood with straight backs and their arms folded. Each one of them were unprofessionally and viciously chewing away on gum. The blue and white police labelled tape marked out a ten-metre squared area. The large fallen tree was there; this was the scene. Matt's visions of reality lapped with those of his dreams, he envisioned the thrashing of the baseball bat against the heads of the victims perfectly.

He slipped back as his foot squelched in some mud. Still crouched, his hand pressed down to break his fall, but a large crack of a branch echoed through towards to the band of police officers. His pair of jeans provided a wiping cloth for his dirty hands as he repositioned to a squatting position. He was precariously close to the scene and at least two of the police officers looked over towards him, about thirty metres away. *Could they see him?* Matt hoped that their vision was obscured. The vast assortment of trees provided sufficient cover, or so Matt thought. The slight stumble had disorientated Matt ever so slightly. One, two, three, four.... A police officer was missing. Matt panicked, getting into trouble with the Police was the last thing he needed. A welcoming handshake at a crime scene wasn't an expectation, but he hadn't really thought about the dire consequences of his actions. He was blinkered by the dreams and the chance of finding an attacker before the police.

It had only been five minutes and cramp began to set in, he hadn't dare move in case of making more noises. *What am I looking for? Give me a sign*, Matt repeatedly thought to himself. The police officers, all four of them had not moved. Their attention had refocussed away from the Matt's location, but nothing was happening.

"Sir, can I help?" A stern but empathetic voice questioned.

Matt jumped up, frightened. The fifth police officer had made an appearance.

"Sorry, ma'am, just out for a walk," Matt wiped his hands again and cracked his knees. He had been hiding out for too long.

"Out for a walk? You're hiding behind bushes near a crime scene," the officer grabbed Matt by the arm. "Come with me, please."

Matt didn't resist and followed the officer through towards the scene of the accident. He could not believe his luck. The snooping he was doing gave no answers but the result of it could be leading somewhere. Rather than take him back to the way he came in, the police officer took him past the crime scene.

"Sergeant Morrison," the officer flashed her card. "What's your name?"

"Matt Crane," he stopped in his tracks about a hundred yards from the crime scene.

The open pathway gave a clearer view of the area. Childhood memories flooded Matt's mind again as he glanced around the area. The tree which was the cause of his own broken collarbone, the boulders that he and Josh used to ambush local walkers from as they walked by, and the background noise of the ravine reminded him of the dams they used to create. He smiled towards Sergeant Morrison in a daze and his vision began to go blurry.

"Matt, are you ok? Stay with us. You can't go yet."

Another wave of sweat overcame Matt as he dipped into an unconsciousness state. The victims of the attack emerged into the area and became visible as Matt looked beyond the large fallen tree. They were too far away to make out who they were, but their stature and clothing made certain that these were the victims.

He couldn't comprehend if this was a dream or not, or how he got in this position. Matt checked himself and looked again, the pair of lovers were linking arms. The police officers had disappeared, and he appeared to have free reign of the woods.

"Matt, Matt. Keep with us," a distant but untraceable voice echoed through the trees.

'I must be unconscious, or at least asleep', Matt thought to himself. It took a moment to realise, but he recognised the voice – it was Sergeant Morrison. He now knew he had limited time as he could be awoken at any time. Looking down in the direction of the narrow tree lined path he could see the attacker approach the couple. The passing of the couple and the attacker was looming. Matt tried to shout at the couple to warn of them of the danger. Nothing. His voice was mute. He looked down and his jeans and jumper had changed to a blue hospital gown. Bewilderment and fear set in as he examined his body. He couldn't talk but he was thinking *'is this the end?'*. At that same moment, a sudden rush of coldness ran through his body and time seemed to slow. He caught a glimpse of someone, his peripheral vision had noted the orange boots and zipped trousers.

Out of nowhere, the orange boot and right foot of the attacker was in front of Matt but the left foot of the attacker was behind Matt. A shimmery outline of the attacker was passing through Matt. The cold worsened as the silhouette of the attacker's body masked through Matt's body. Matt had often wondered what a near death experience felt like, the unanimous light at the end of tunnel seemed like a fairy-tale myth compared to this. A split second passed but at the same time it was long enough to think of family and friends. Time to think about the victims and the attacker of this crime.

The attacker gradually continued his walk, just like that of the dream. Only it was slower. This was different to the dream; the attacker tilted his head – the face still not visible but he was beginning to turn, and face Matt. Matt began to get nervous and the sky began to get brighter. The turning of the attacker's head was in sync with the sun coming out from the behind the clouds. Matt clutched his neck for split second as the attacker grabbed him. It was brief but still frightening.

"He's got a pulse and he's breathing."

"I think he's just passed out."

"The ambulance is on its way."

A couple of the other police officer's joined Sergeant Morrison in propping up Matt against an old oak tree.

"I'm... I am ok. I don't need an ambulance," Matt croaked and coughed.

He rubbed his eyes and face. His hands were covered in mud and it contributed further to the dirt already on his face. Matt held out his hand in front of him at an angle to assess his nerves. He could see the veins through the back of his hand throb and thump to each quick heartbeat.

"How long was out I for?" Matt took to his feet and checked his watch. It was still seven thirty and still broken. His vision was blurry from the sweat and he was still uneasy on his feet.

"I think you should sit back down; you were out for twenty minutes."

The other two police officers went back to man the crime scene as Sergeant Morrison tried to comfort Matt. Brushing off his trousers and dusting himself down, Matt was desperate to get a glimpse of the scene.

"Sir, where are you going, you can't go over there. You'll disturb the crime scene," Sergeant Morrison tried to grab Matt by the arm, but her clasp slipped. "You fell flat on your face, you need help."

"I just need a quick a look and I'll be gone. I don't need any help," Matt whimpered and stumbled closer to crime scene.

Each squelch of mud got quicker as Matt started to regain consciousness and stability in his legs. He twisted and cranked his neck to stretch but it triggered a shooting pain through his skull. The same two police officers from earlier pulled across to try and block access to the crime scene.

There was nothing to see, he could easily peer over and around the police officers. A fallen tree, a few footprints and remnants of blood splatter soaked into the dead leaves and mud. All marked out with numbered yellow flags.

"Your neck and shoulder too. That looks like a nasty gash," Sergeant Morrison had caught up to Matt.

Matt checked his neck, his jacket had rolled down and exposed a three-inch wound. Blood was slowly seeping down his arm and mixing with the drying mud on the palm of his hand. He glanced up to Sergeant Morrison and back down to his arm several times.

The eyes of Matt locked into Sergeant Morrison's sky-blue eyes and his lips quivered, "I did this the other day; I fell down the stairs so the wound must have just re-opened from the fall."

Sergeant Morrison nodded in belief, but Matt had also convinced himself that it had been cut by the fall on the stairs. He zipped up his jacket, soaking up the last bits of blood in the process. He knew he couldn't remember if the cut was from the fall on the stairs. He woke up with the cut on his neck and convinced himself it was from the stairs. Only now, he starts to think that he is receiving physical signs from the dream.

Matt rubbed his neck as he tried to link the attack to his cut. Looking over to the crime scene didn't induce any more thoughts or give any answers. It just raised more questions. *What is going on here? What I am looking for?* Matt's mind was in overdrive.

"Those prints. They're the attackers, an orange pair of boots… and… and he came from that way," Matt pointed to the original entrance that he wanted to come through.

"How would you know that sir?" Sergeant Morrison quizzed Matt.

"The blow came from a baseball bat. Black stripes on it," Matt couldn't stop himself. "And he left with a female who was originally with the victim".

The voice of Matt escalated frantically as he blurted details of his dream. All the commotion had attracted the attention of the other police officers.

"Sir, you need to come with us. You're unfit to travel and you need some medical attention."

"No, I'm fine. I need to go home. Why have you still got this police tape up? It happened ages ago, there is nothing more to see."

"Fanboys. Sick fanboys. You're not one of them, are you?" Sergeant Morrison asked and followed Matt to the main entrance of the woods. "Why are you coming up with these theories and snooping around?"

Matt could not muster up a response. His mind was all over the place and his body was in pieces. He was aching from head to toe and his head felt like it could explode. Trees covered this area of the entrance in huge quantities. The perfect place for somebody to enter and leave without anybody else seeing. Matt embraced the surroundings, taking in each detail of the trees and undergrowth – painting a picture within his mind.

He sifted through his pockets to retrieve his car keys and dropped them into a pile of dead leaves whilst panicking.

"Sir, we can't force you, but you should wait for this ambulance."

Picking up his keys, Matt shook his head. The creak of the swinging gate was followed by a big thud as it slammed against the frame. The coy, novice police officer who had let him in the woods earlier on, stepped back to let him jog across the car park and back towards his vehicle.

"That's his car? Why did you let him in?" Sergeant Morrison asked PC Phillips.

Phillips didn't reply, still embarrassed and still learning the ropes. Her silence was broken as Matt swiftly reversed his car, kicking up dust and desperate to get away.

"Send his plates to the office and get a tail on him," asked Sergeant Morrison as she stared intensely at Matt's departing vehicle.

"Why didn't you arrest him ma'am? He seemed shifty," PC Phillips replied as she radioed through with Matt's registration and a tracking request to the office.

"For what? You have a lot to learn, Phillips," Sergeant Morrison turned away and pulled her jacket in towards her body. "Just follow it up and get back to me."

CHAPTER 6

Solving a crime with dreams would set a precedent. Nostradamus territory. Bringing this up without any real information or evidence would sound crazy and it did. Matt knew deep down that he would be mocked and ostracised if he publicly claimed to know details of the crime without being there. *Had the adrenaline from the passing out in the woods led to the outburst of information to the police?* Matt began to wonder.

A passing ambulance with full lights and sirens whizzed past Matt as he headed home. He had managed to calm down and was driving at a steady pace but still clutching the steering wheel with his clammy hands. The internal mirror provided a reflection to check the aftereffects of his diluted pupils, he was on the mend. It also displayed what was behind his car. A further sense of clam came over him as he realised that he wasn't being followed.

Why did you do it and *you're next*, Matt kept over thinking the words of the attacker. Lapses of trepidation instigated quick glances into each of the side mirrors before a tense stare through the internal mirror. Still no tail but Matt was getting paranoid.

Matt began to brace himself for Helen's interrogation as he pulled the car onto the driveway. It was still morning and he could see Helen through the living room working in the back office.

The weed filled pathway to the front door preoccupied Matt's mind as he tried to make a plan of action. Shower and bed – then avoid Helen.

"Hey, it's just me. I'm jumping in the shower," Matt shouted through to Helen.

"I've got a conference call in ten minutes, so I'll be busy for the next couple of hours," she shouted back. "Are you ok?"

"Yea, I'm good. Just took a silly tumble in woods but it's just my pride that's damaged," he glanced down at his jeans. "Well and a bit muddy too."

Matt flipped off his boots and scurried halfway up the stairs to the bathroom. He looked over the bannister for any clues as to where he might have cut his neck. Nothing was obvious as he rubbed the palm of his hand across the bannister and stairs.

The nineteenth century mirror at the top of the stairs was impossible to avoid but Matt managed to keep contact to a minimum. It was still enough time to notice that his clothes and face were still covered in mud. He was half right in telling Helen that his pride was hurt. It wasn't the fall that was frustrating him.

I need a real lead, Matt thought to himself as he stripped down and turned the shower on. Water dripped down as he stepped over the bath panel and under the shower head. The shower was near scolding, but he hadn't noticed. He stared towards the base of the shower basin, watching the water whirl into the plug when he noticed a stream of blood. The sight of blood prompted a little yelp as the hot water intensified. He reached to the temperature gauge in desperation and took it down a notch. The neck wound had reopened again, albeit slightly cleaner this time.

"Are you ok?" Helen was sat on the toilet next to him in the bathroom. "Your neck again?"

"Jesus, you made me jump," Matt held his arm out on the glass screen. "I thought you were in a conference."

"Ten-minute delay," Helen finished up her wee and pulled down her dress. "The cut on your neck?"

"It's just re-opened from that fall on the stairs. It's not deep, just an annoying graze that won't stop bleeding."

"Well, get a dressing on it. There's some in the medicine cupboard," Helen said as she headed back downstairs.

The medicine cupboard was a cauldron of drugs and plasters of years gone by. Matt wrapped a towel around his waist and examined the cupboard for a dressing. The headache was still present, so he simultaneously looked for some painkillers.

"Fentanyl?" he whispered to himself.

He quickly dressed his neck and disposed of the wrapper in the bin. Matt was desperate to go to sleep. The resulting feeling from passing out and subsequent headache were one reason, but the possibility of another dream was also an inviting prospect.

The Fentanyl packet was still in date. Presumably, Helen's. Well, he knew they were not his but wondered why she would have had such a strong painkiller. He couldn't recall any trauma or issues she had in recent times. *Well, there is some left so it could not have been that bad*, he thought.

Emptying the toothbrush holder, he filled it up with bathroom tap water and threw two tablets into his mouth. He gulped down the cup of water and headed to the bedroom. The towel dropped from his waist as he climbed into bed. The packet of Fentanyl was still in his hand.

Take one tablet, once a day, with food.

Matt shrugged as he acknowledged his multiple wrongdoings.

"Matt, come on downstairs," Helen shouted from downstairs.

He quickly chucked the empty packet of Fentanyl to one side and got dressed. A smart freshly ironed shirt with a pair of black jeans were laid out on the end of the bed. Helen must have prepared them as Matt was only good with the golf version of an iron.

"Yea hurry up. Or else I'll beat your ass!" A husky voice followed up.

Matt instantly recognised the voice. It was his brother; Josh. Perplexity was drawn across Matt's face as he headed down the stairs and through to the living room whilst still tucking his shirt. Helen had left her office and was sat on the sofa with Josh and Amy. Helen's parents were wedged together on the adjacent love seat.

"What's going on? Have I missed a birthday?" Matt laughed.

"We're just here for you that's all. Remember, we love you no matter what," Helen comforted Matt.

Matt took a step back as he tried to understand what was going on, "Where's that draft coming from?" Matt looked around; he knew there was no air conditioning, but it felt like a clean, fresh breeze. The doors were shut, and the curtains were drawn.

Matt looked at each of the group with a blank expression as nobody replied. The pouffe was empty so Matt lifted his jeans from his thighs and took a seat. Despite the greeting, the atmosphere was less than welcoming and there was an obvious sense of anxiety in the air.

"The police. They want to talk. We want to talk," Josh leant forward and looked Matt dead in the eye.

"About what? I need a drink," Matt worried.

It wasn't uncommon for Matt to run away from his problems. Matt was hopeful of getting an answer from the bottom of a cup of tea. Nobody followed him into the kitchen and there was no further voice, just the sound of a boiling kettle providing an atmospheric kitchen.

The boiling kettle was nearing the end, the bubbling of the water was leading to the inevitable blip of the kettle switch to confirm completion. But it carried on. Matt flipped the switch up and down, but it didn't stop boiling – the water was beginning to come out of the spout as a shadow formed at the kitchen door.

Matt turned to see who it was, "Josh?"

"Don't worry about it. Everything will be fine," Josh sounded like he was begging. "Just know that we'll always be here for you."

"For Christ sake, what are you on about?"

The boiling water gushed from the kettle and poured onto Matt's hand. An ear shrieking scream echoed the room as his hand instantly blistered and went red.

"Matt, Matt. Wake up," Helen was shaking his shoulders as he sweated profusely.

Matt sat up in his bed as Helen held his back. He held up his hand to check for a burn but there was nothing.

"We need to get you to the hospital. This isn't normal," Helen rubbed his back as he twisted his body to let his legs hang out of the bed.

The initial light-headedness was fading, and Matt began to collect his feelings again. He held out the palms of his hands and turned them around. He glanced at the dressing on his neck in the wall length mirror and the towel was still strewn across the bedroom floor.

"I've just had another bad dream. Don't worry about it," he stood up confidently. He was naked but stood with strength to show Helen he was ok.

"About the crime again?"

"No, Just the usual weird stuff this time."

Helen was surprised that any other dream could be stranger than the crime associated ones but then she noticed the Fentanyl on the side. She picked up the empty packet and shook her head. Matt knew he shouldn't have taken them and refused to say anything.

He grabbed the towel and dabbed himself down before spraying a copious amount of deodorant. The jeans and shirt from the dream were on the edge of the bed so he began to dress himself. It made him think that although he doesn't consciously see things, he must absorb them into his memory. It was only adding further doubt to his other dreams.

"I think we should call off the meal with your brother and Amy," Helen said.

"No, I'm fine. I'm sure this will all blow over soon. The police sound like they're on top of things and I reckon my dreams will die down once they've caught somebody."

Helen passed him the empty packet of Fentanyl, "There were two in here. Have you had both?"

"Yea, I thought they'd help," Matt sheepishly replied.

"No wonder you've been asleep for six hours."

"Six hours!?" Matt looked at the alarm clock. She was right.

"We best get going soon," Matt added.

"I've come up to get dressed. Work is done," Helen opened her wardrobe pulled out a red dress.

"You'll look beautiful. I'll be downstairs."

The jog downstairs didn't trigger any memory of the cut. Matt rolled up the sleeves of his checked shirt, Helen won't be happy with the creases. The dressing on his neck was seeped in blood. An infection was the last thing Matt needed so he headed into the kitchen for the first aid kit. He had only taken four steps upon passing the side window. An unfamiliar car was parked across the road. Matt leant into the window frame with his hands pressed down into the sill to focus on the vehicle.

A black BMW. An unmarked police car. The police can never really be inconspicuous, as much as they try. A male figure was sat in the driver's seat, alone in the car. Intense eye contact led to the driver starting the engine and slowly leaving the side of the road.

Matt know knew that the police had tailed him from the crime scene. He stood biting his nails, overthinking everything he had gone through. The car had long gone but it didn't stop Matt making a delayed dash to the front door. An adrenaline fuelled sprint down the footpath to the main road attracted the attention of the nearby neighbour who was gardening.

"Did you see that car, Norma?"

"Yes, he was watching your house. Are you ok?" A dainty old woman replied. "That was a police officer, you know."

The old lady brushed the hair from her forehead before resting both hands against her hips. Proud of her investigative work.

There was a long pause. Matt didn't want to incriminate himself, so he ignored her and returned to the footpath to his house.

"Is everything ok?" she yelled as he opened and closed the front door behind him.

Matt slumped to the floor with his back against the door. His heartrate had risen, reminiscent of when he was in car park at the woods. The last thing he wanted was the nosey neighbour snooping out of her window and spreading rumours to the others on the street.

"What's up?" Helen asked. "Are you ok?"

Matt held his head in his hands, "not really."

He pushed himself up from the floor, he was beginning to waver. His body looked as though he hadn't slept in days and his mind was elsewhere for the most part.

"Come on, let's have a quick drink before we go over to Josh and Amy's house," Helen kissed Matt and herded him into the living room as she headed to the kitchen.

"These beers are warm, that ok?" she shouted from the kitchen.

Matt was stood at the living room window looking down the street assessing the area. The curtain of Norma's living room quickly dropped and began to shake. He didn't see her, but he knew her curious old mind was in action.

"Did you see that?" Matt said as he paced the room. "The police followed me from the crime scene."

Helen entered the living room, beer in one hand and wine in the other. She seemed calm; outside of work was much easier for the pair of them. The atmosphere of the household was a much more pleasant place without the stress of Helen's job. Helen's law work and career was a common argument between them, it was pretty much the only thing they would have disagreements about. The quarrels always led to the question of kids and when they were having them.

"That car back is back again," Helen sipped her wine, a Sauvignon Blanc, whilst looking out of the bay window.

"So, you did it see it!" Matt shouted, "And this beer is warm."

Matt rushed to the main light switch to brighten up the room and then dashed to the front door. A last second decision to go to the door rather than the window. Fumbling with the key lock he managed to get out and down the footpath. The darkness of the night lit up in front of him as Norma's outdoor turned light on. He couldn't help but notice that she was peering through the window, but his focus switched to that of the car.

Spotting the latch off the gate, he skipped through to the road, but it was too late. The car tyres screeched and skidded before it accelerated up and off the cul-de-sac, again.

Matt stood in the middle of the road, panting as though he had completed a marathon. He wiped his brow, no sweat but he looked lost. But then he saw Norma who had now moved to her front door.

"The police again," she shook her head.

Matt didn't entertain her and brushed her off with swipe of his arm in her direction. The latch had broken on his garden gate, he fiddled with it for a couple of seconds but then remembered that he had more pressing matters.

Helen greeted him entering the house, "What have you been up to?"

"Come on, we need to go now before that car comes back," Matt grabbed his jacket from the end of the bannister, "I'll explain on the way."

"No, you need..."

"No! We need to go. Now."

Helen took Matt's frantic actions seriously and rushed back into the living room for her black handbag and faux-fur coat. She saw that Matt was frightened and needed a drink for herself; she gulped the last of her wine and checked through her bag to make sure she had the essentials.

CHAPTER 7

Matt was sat waiting in Helen's car. It wasn't going to deter the police from following them but at least they had some comfort.

"The police can't watch you and then storm off. It doesn't make sense," Helen slammed the door of the car and wrapped the seatbelt across. "Are you sure it's the police?"

"Yea. I saw the hidden lights and the driver had that stern demeanour about them. You know what I mean?"

"If you say so. Just get us to your brother's house in one piece."

He gripped the steering wheel and shifted through the gears. Cases like this were unheard of in this part of the country, never mind Alice Hills. Matt thought deeply as his eyes paced to each wing mirror.

"Calm down, you're going to get us hurt. What have you done?" Helen placed a calming hand over his as he grabbed the gearstick.

It was almost instant, his nerves and heartrate lowered. He could feel and hear inner words from Helen as he refocussed on the road ahead – *everything will be ok.*

The road to Josh's house was dimly lit, just the moonlight and car headlights to guide the way. Being a local was beneficial as he was basically driving blind.

"Wow, those are bright, who is that?" Matt noticed a car speeding to the rear of his car. "They're not slowing down either."

Helen bent forward to peer into her side mirror, "you're right. Take a left down Broad Street. Nobody ever goes down there."

Matt didn't use the indicator and took the turning as late as possible. He patiently looked into the rear-view mirror again. Lights; two bright lights entered the road. They were being followed.

"Shit, the police. It's that damn BMW again. What are they doing?" Matt said.

"Just go to your brothers house. Look I'm a lawyer, the police around here aren't competent. This case has triggered all sorts of naivety," Helen tried to reassure Matt.

Matt slowed down beneath the speeding limit. He didn't want to give a reason for them to pull him over. Broad Street looped back around to the main road and Matt continued. The following car had dropped back, both vehicles were now sure of the pursuit.

"So, come on. I've asked more than once. What have you done?" Helen demanded.

"I've not done anything," Matt squealed in a high pitch voice. A clear sign that he was hiding something, and it triggered Helen's eye brows to rise in disbelief.

"I passed out..."

"What? Again? We are going straight to the hospital after this meal."

"I'm fine. I'm fine," it was Matt's turn for reassurance.

Matt couldn't help but notice that the following vehicle was getting closer again, like a predator closing in on its prey.

"You're right about the police though. They don't have a clue what to do," Matt added.

"So, why are they following you? Why are they following us? I have a career to think about."

Matt was shocked that she cared more about her work than his welfare and he made it known to her.

"Sorry, I didn't mean it like that. I love you," Helen lifted Matt's hand and kissed the back of it.

"I just wanted to look at the scene. I'm surprised they let me so close to it."

Helen wasn't surprised, "Like I said, they're inept."

"This passing out episode was different," Matt gripped the steering wheel tighter. "It felt like I was at the scene. I saw the victims, but I couldn't shout."

Helen checked the mirror again; she could see the following vehicle was getting closer and double checked that her seatbelt was tightly fastened. Matt saw the tension and reacted similarly. Helen backtracked and consoled Matt again, this time both hands across the back of his hand. She needed her driver to be relaxed at the wheel.

"The attacker was there. Dressed the same. J Hat, orange boots, everything. His body went through me like a ghost. I felt the cold. One slight difference though. The police let slip that there was only one victim but…"

"But what?" Helen interjected. She could sense he was going to spin his own narrative on the whole thing.

"Never mind," Matt started to question himself.

"Ok, give me more. Did you see his face?"

"No, it was the same. Blurry with a beard."

"Everybody has beards in this town. You, your brother, and all your friends have beards. Including Ade," Helen listed the names on her fingers.

She was right. The hipster generation all looked the same. Matt knew that everybody was going through a phase of trying to look trendy. The J hat matched with a beard was a perfect disguise. Hide in plain sight. There was nothing original about the looks of the attacker and Matt knew it.

Matt thought about all of his friends, "Maybe you're right. Maybe I'm going mad and I'm just painting the dreams with all of my memories. This is just a coincidence."

"You've still dreamed about it though. But what have you done to make them tail us?" Helen encouraged him to carry on. She wanted to know what trouble he had got himself into. Although a sense of curiosity was still lingering about the dream and its link to the crime.

"Erm, I just told them what the attacker was wearing and where they walked to and from."

"What!?" Helen could not believe her ears. "You have no evidence. Do you not realise you have just made yourself suspect number one?"

Matt quickly realised what she meant. He hadn't given it a thought. His so-called assistance was a help for the police but not in the way he thought.

Helen could see the cogs in Matt's mind going round in circles, "You have turned up at the crime scene and told them details of the crime," she took a deep breath. "Some of which they already know, because of, you know, real evidence. The rest you have made up from your dream which could coincidentally be true."

The rage in Helen's face was evident as she continued, "how can you be so stupid? How do you not realise?"

"I don't know, I just wanted to help."

"You better hope that no more evidence or any other case details match to those of your dream. Otherwise you'll be sleeping in a cell, in no time."

Helens' anger shifted to disbelief. Her job requires evidence-based facts. She knew that the police couldn't charge him with anything, but if some of the detail of his dream matched the detail of the crime then they would have probable cause to investigate and arrest him.

"They don't know that you have dreamed up this information. They wouldn't believe that anyway," Helen broke the silence again.

"They will. They're clues and they'll help them."

Helen couldn't quite believe how ridiculous he was being, "your visions are short sighted. You're only looking at people you know for a start. An investigator doesn't do that."

"I know, but the clues I'm seeing are with people we know."

"I wouldn't exactly call them clues."

Matt shrugged and checked his mirror again, "ow!".

"Are you ok? Watch the road."

"I can't. The light is too bright."

The lights of the following vehicle had intensified. Full beams had been switched on and they radiated into Matt's eyes through the central mirror.

"Slow down then," Helen was beginning to think they were going to crash.

Matt covered his left eye with his left hand and noticed that he could see. The light was beaming directly into one eye. Driving one handed was not exactly sensible, especially considering Matt's track record of crashes. Previous accidents flashed before Helen's eyes as she sat clutching her seat beat. She pulled Matt's hand away from his face.

"Slow down and concentrate," Helen screamed.

Both cars were swaying all over the road, but Matt decided Helen was right. If the police were really following them then they would have pulled him over by now. They were nearing the safety of Josh's house and Matt would have the physical attributes of Josh to help him.

Matt looked up at the mirror again, "Jeez, my other eye."

The lights began to flash but the focus was now into his right eye. He winced and turned his ahead away from the mirror, but the light deepened and began to burn his eye. A shake of the head immediately withdrew the light and he managed to refocus on the road.

Helen and Matt looked at each other in shock. They both thought the same thing as the lights dwindled away into the darkness.

"They've gone. Why? They can't be the police," Helen's head swivelled left and right to double check.

The engine began to simmer as the speed of the car drastically slowed.

"Wait until I get into work tomorrow. I'm ringing Alice Hills police and giving them a piece of my mind," Helen was furious.

She slammed the door shut; Matt hadn't even come to a complete stop but the adrenaline stabilised her. Even in the high heels she chose to wear she showed great balance. Matt grabbed his jacket off the back seat to bide some time. It wasn't like he needed the jacket; they were staying indoors all night.

"Don't talk about what has just happened," Helen dusted herself down as she pressed the doorbell. "We're guests."

Matt casually nodded. The crime case and Matt's mental state had both developed quite drastically since Matt was last at Josh and Amy's house. He knew that Josh would take the mickey out of him, the possibility of a police interrogation would be highly amusing for Josh. No brotherly love loss here.

"Hey guys, come on in," Josh opened the door and grabbed Matt's jacket before directing them towards the kitchen.

Amy was stood behind Josh and gave a warm smile before heading to the kitchen to make some drinks.

Josh checked outside and peered left and right in a jovial manner, "so, no near misses tonight then?"

Helen stared at Matt and he gulped in response. She had a clear expression of concern on her face, *had he seen the chase?*

"Oh, no not today," Matt laughed.

Matt suddenly realised that Josh was referring to the Lorry that nearly hit him. Or him nearly hitting the lorry, it depends which perspective Josh was taking.

Helen shook her head and went to help Amy finish up in the kitchen. She didn't want to hear another story from Matt.

"Bit tense. Are you both ok?" Josh questioned Matt but then proceeded with a spring in his step as he led Matt into the living room.

"We're both ok, this dream and crime nonsense has gone a bit too far."

"You haven't conked out again have you?"

Amy and Helen entered the living room and handed out some beers.

"Me and Amy will have a bit of girl chat through here. You guys put the football on," Helen tried to change to the subject to save Matt's embarrassment.

"How long have you had a BMW for?" Matt swigged half the bottle of his beer as he looked out of the living room window.

"Just a few days, beautiful ride. Fancy a quick go before you have any more beer?"

Matt slammed the beer down and headed straight to the door. He hadn't noticed the BMW on the way in. The stress and fluster from the chase distracted him. The door was locked but Matt grabbed the keys from the side and unlocked it himself.

"Somebody is a little excited. You do know it's not a Ferrari," Josh couldn't keep up with Matt.

Matt staggered down a few steps and onto the large double driveway. Helen's Mercedes lined up against Josh's BMW, two black and beautiful motors. As a car salesman, Matt didn't need to sell these types of cars, they sold themselves. The passion for cars was usually missing for Matt, he didn't overly care, and Josh knew this. So, Josh was not only surprised but slightly disturbed when he came out of the house to see Matt pressing his face and hands against the bonnet of the car.

Matt stepped back to gauge a mental note of the BMW temperature and moved over to the Mercedes. He did the same thing to Helen's car which was much warmer as he couldn't hold his hands there for too long. Going back and forth between the cars didn't help, the transfer of heat was making each car feel the same.

"Are we driving the car or just hugging it?" Josh shook the keys to get his attention but didn't find the situation strange.

"When did you last drive this car? Pop the bonnet," Matt quizzed Josh and tried to justify the bonnet hugging.

"I just went the shop for the beers earlier on."

Matt tried to open the driver's side door as he circled the car. He was starting to show genuine interest in the car but the underlying agenda of whether it was the one that had been following him was eating away at him.

"The bonnet, not the boot," Matt said as he passed the rear of the car.

Josh was fiddling with the keys, it only had two buttons, but he was struggling with the technology of it all. Shaking his head, Matt peered into the boot for a curious browse and noticed a bright pair of orange boots stood upright on a plastic bag. The mud on the boots was still fresh.

"Nice boots," Matt wanted to a trigger a response without a blunt question.

"Oh, they're not mine. The previous owner left them in. But yea, nice boots," Josh quickly shut the boot sheepishly.

Josh pressed the central locking again to allow Matt to get in as he couldn't work out how to open the bonnet.

"Nice ride," Matt was slightly distracted with the thought of the orange boots as he nestled into the bucket seat of the BMW.

Matt took a moment to compose himself and thought back of the good times with Josh. Josh always had Matt's back no matter what. Pub scuffles, Josh was always there to help him out. School problems and detentions, Josh covered for him.

Why would Josh chase me? I can't contemplate him coming after me. Mum and dad would be so angry for me thinking like this, Matt slipped into a small daydream as he thought further about what he was doing.

"Boys, come on. The food is out," Helen shouted from the front door.

"Maybe next time, eh," Josh held the door of the car open.

"Definitely. Nought to Sixty in three point eight seconds, plenty of miles to gallon and perfect traction."

"I've already bought it, brother. You don't need your salesman pitch with me," Josh clipped him around the head and got him in a head lock.

They laughed and joked on the way to the kitchen. Helen and Amy smiled as they sipped away on their wine, they were happy to see the brothers getting on. Helen was particularly glad to see Matt acting normal. If only for a moment.

Amy and Helen had set up the table perfectly; fresh beers, cutlery and a mouth-watering layout of food. Pizza, chicken, kebabs and salad. A quality range of buffet food to graze on. Some twenty minutes of idle chat passed between them all. Light-hearted conversations really eased the atmosphere and it was just what they all needed, especially Matt. He had calmed himself down and forgot about all of his issues, the love was coasting through the room.

"You should already know that I have a BMW," Josh crunched into some pizza crust.

"BMW?" Helen coughed and nearly choked on her red wine. She hadn't noticed the type of the vehicle.

Amy grabbed some kitchen roll to wipe up the small spill that Helen had caused. Helen smiled as a thank you, but she looked at Matt who shook his head – trying to get her to forget about the car chase and BMW.

The discomfort of Helen's posture eased off. The jerk reaction from the announcement of a BMW caused a short shooting pain through her spine. She looked down at her glass and then back to Matt. It was her time to be embarrassed. Thousands of BMW's are on the roads of Britain, probably a hundred of which are in the small town of Alice Hills, and Helen found herself linking Josh to the chasing car and the crime.

I can't fall into Matt's way of thinking; he's rubbing off on me, she thought to herself as she smiled at Josh and Amy at the table.

"Yea, a BMW. Cool car, eh Matt?" Josh was wolfing down the food like he hadn't eaten for a week.

"Beautiful, but why would I know you have one?"

"I bought it from your mate at work. Ade, I think he is called?"

"No, he didn't say. We sell a lot of them though."

"This one was his own, not from the showroom. He really knows his cars, you know. You could a learn a lot from him," Josh let out a slight belch as he washed down some food with a beer.

"He has a 4X4," Matt questioned himself.

Amy and Helen had long left the conversation and were chatting between themselves. They got on like a house on fire, like the real sister they both never had. They often joked that they would always be friends no matter what, even if their partners split from them. These sort of conservations usually took place over a bottle of wine or two, but drunk talk always seemed to be truthful and make the most sense.

"Yea, he told me all about that 4X4 but he loves picking up the ladies in his BMW," Josh laughed. "His words not mine. Anyway he needed to shift it and I was happy to oblige."

"I thought he only had one car. The work 4X4," Matt bit his nails. It wasn't long before his mind was back thinking about the case.

"Obviously not, eh," Josh left the table to scramble his way through towards the fridge and Amy followed him, leaving Matt to his thoughts.

"So, the orange boots are Ade's?" Matt asked.

"Boots?" Josh paused for a second. "Oh yea, Ade's. I need to drop them off."

"I suppose I could take…"

"No, just let Josh take them back," Helen intersected the conversation knowing that any further involvement with Ade would be disastrous.

The snapping interruption from Helen dropped the mood slightly and Amy gave Josh a perplexed look. Plenty of food and drink was consumed over the next couple of minutes as they all tried to summon up the courage to start the conversation again.

Amy looked at Josh numerous times but only got his attention by knocking the table leg and creating a noise. *'Now?'* Amy mimed her mouth towards him, and he nodded back.

Helen peered over to see what they were up to, but a pillar blocked her view. She could hear murmurs and squabbles between them which prompted her to look at Matt. She had deep-rooted love for her husband and any teething problems they were having were nothing in comparison to their devotion for each other.

"We've got some exciting news," Josh carried over a few glasses of Champagne.

The love on Helen's face towards to Matt switched to the direction of Josh and Amy. Without any second thought, Helen knew exactly what this news was and took a sip of Amy's drink. It wasn't wine.

"We're having a baby!"

Josh handed over the half-filled glasses of champagne and gave Amy a kiss. Amy was her usual quiet self but her beaming smile teamed with a rub of her blossoming tummy signalled obvious joy.

"Congratulations," Matt stepped in and shook and his brother's hand. "Amy," he followed up with a nod.

Matt couldn't help but be jealous. He was happy for them both, but it was something he wanted, and his younger brother had beaten him to it. Helen whisked herself around the table and gave Amy a big hug. She was ecstatic, she knew Amy was desperate for a baby and the announcement was both a joy and relief.

"We've been trying for over a year. We can't believe it. It was such a surprise that it had finally happened," Josh said.

Matt was shocked at Helen's response. He had mithered her for a family for over a year and she had always been dismissive. Josh could sense the slight disappointment in Matt's face and put his arm around his shoulders.

"Your time will come. It will. Hopefully, this will get Helen broody," Josh whispered into Matt's ear.

"I'm sorry, I'm spoiling this for you," Matt realised he was being a jerk. "I really am happy for you both, let's have a toast."

They all raised a glass and gave a smile as they looked each other in the eye.

Matt raised the glass further, "I'm going to be an uncle."

They all laughed, seeing Matt less serious was good to see. His obsession with the crime and his dreams had begun to take over his life. Helen noticed he was more relaxed and moved over to embrace him. She whispered into his ear; her lips slightly brushed against his lobe – she promised him that they would try for baby soon.

The whisper felt like an out of body experience and Matt's mind drifted into a cloud like serenity and closed his eyes. For a few seconds, his body was at ease and a sudden rush of peace raced through his body.

He re-opened his eyes, his vision slightly blurred as his sight tried to adjust again. Matt instantly locked onto the bookshelf and directly to the infertility book that he saw a couple of days ago. It was unclear who had the fertility issues, and it was prudent to ask over such sensitive matter. Either way, seeing the book reaffirmed the cause for celebration.

"Honestly mate, I'm really chuffed for you and Amy," Matt had moved from the wine and onto his beer, and clinked bottles.

"I appreciate it brother. I didn't think I could. We tried all sorts with the doctors. It was me having all the tests and then bang," Josh slapped the back of his hand.

Matt was a little shocked, Josh had never told him about any issues. The thought of asking why he hadn't said anything in the past did cross Matt's mind but he knew that Josh would probably be silent about it with his macho image. Helen and Amy were sat in the living room both giggling to each other with the television on in the background.

"What are you two laughing at?" Josh asked as he and Matt jumped on the sofa.

"You can clean that up," Helen pointed to the spilt beer.

Glancing at the floor, Matt noticed a small pool of beer. It wasn't even Helen's house and she was ordering Matt around. Josh laughed as Matt pried himself up and off the sofa and made his way to the kitchen in an embarrassed fashion.

The good news had really lightened up the mood and Matt could hear them all joke and laugh as they came up with ideas and silly baby names. He took the time out to quickly tidy up the kitchen. The bin was full, the infertility book rested on top. Josh had not wasted anytime in getting rid of that, he must have seen Matt looking at.

"Hey Matt, get in here. Crime Watch is on," Josh shouted.

Matt rushed into the living room, tea towel still in his hand from cleaning up.

"What's this?" Matt asked as he cleaned up the spilt beer.

He looked over his shoulder at Helen. She gave a short shake of the head with raised eyebrows, clearly not impressed with what Josh was about to show Matt.

"It's this crime up in Alice Hills. It's gone national. The whole country is going to know about your dream," Josh gave Matt a couple of digs to the ribs.

"Oh yea, they mentioned something on the radio earlier today," Matt replied.

It suddenly dawned on Matt that this was serious. He checked back again to Helen, she was crunched forward, arms folded with a worried face. They may have all joked in the past about Matt dreaming about the crime but his actions at the crime scene had spiked concern, to Helen anyway. And, despite his lack of real understanding, Josh could also sense something was wrong.

"Are you both ok?" Josh asked as the opening credits and theme tune played on the TV.

"This fool turned up at the crime scene and told police about his dream," Helen pointed to Matt in anger. "I'm sorry Amy, I'll be calm."

"Really?" Josh laughed more. "Well that's you being suspect number one."

Matt felt a sickness inside his stomach. His so-called stupid brother worked out the consequences of Matt's actions within seconds. He looked at Amy knowing any distress or commotion wasn't good. *I'm sorry*, he mimed.

"I didn't think. I just thought that I was helping. And anyway, I only told them the details, I never mentioned anything about having a dream."

"That doesn't exactly make things any better," replied Josh. "It probably makes things worse."

Josh was being too honest which caused Matt more worry. Matt sat down next Josh again and took a swig of his beer as the TV presenter prepared to introduce the programme. All four of them were glued to the TV screen as mixed emotions aired through the room.

"Good evening, Sarah Tunson here, welcome to Crime Watch. We start with Northern England tonight. A quaint little town called Alice Hills."

The endearing tone of the female presenter really set scene as she proceeded to paint the picture of Alice Hills and details of the case. Sarah Tunson was mid-forties, or certainly looked it. The quantity of make-up layered upon a cosmetic ridden face would often leave the viewers at home questioning the image of most TV presenters rather than the subject of the show. Crime Watch and Sarah were no different.

"It is rare for this to happen, but the local police of Alice Hills asked us earlier today to present this case. The last pieces of evidence were submitted just fifteen minutes before the start of the show. They are, we are, desperate to get things moving on this sickening attack," Sarah Tunson brushed her sleek brown hair to one side and shuffled her file of papers which were only there for dramatic effects.

"Come on then," Matt had virtually crawled to the front of the TV, desperate for more information.

"Your eyes will go square," Josh laughed as he mimicked their dad's voice and Matt retreated back to the sofa.

Sarah moved across the TV set where the national news anchor, Jim Jones, presided next to a graphics board. Jim was a national treasure, older than most people could remember. He was way past the traditional retirement age, but the public loved him. The TV channel also loved the ratings he brought.

"Jim."

"Hi Sarah."

"What have you got for us?"

Jim panned to the camera. The concern on his face and the slight hesitation indicated the seriousness of this case. A model professional like Jim wouldn't usually stutter on camera.

"We have one victim. Male. Late thirties. He was wearing black gloves and a black hat matched together with a green jacket and black trousers."

"This sounds like a basic description considering the cold elements of Alice Hills," Sarah raised the tone of what started out as a nothing story.

"Well, we have to keep the details of the victim quiet for the time being to protect their safety – they are currently in a coma but signs are looking good for a recovery. What we can say is that the victim entered the woods from the south side with a female companion. This female companion was dressed the same. But, after the attack, the female left the scene with the attacker."

"How do we know this, Jim?"

"A dog walker who also entered the south side of the woods gave a statement confirming a male and female dressed the same walked by them with arms together – smitten. Dress like this on your own and you wouldn't stand out, but two people dressed identical makes people notice. For this dog walker anyway." He pointed to a photograph of plain, unbranded clothing on the digital board but there was nothing striking about the outfits.

"I told you that there was a dog walker," Matt clapped his hands.

Jim Jones flicked over the graphic with his remote control, *"a search of the area confirms two pairs of prints walking through from the south end of the woods to the scene of the attack."*

The images on the screen, taken by the police, showed two clear lines of footprints in sync with another. It was obvious that the producers of the footprints were walking together.

"Now, this is where it gets interesting," Jim did his best to seduce the viewers. "The victim took a single strike to the back of the head with a blunt instrument and was left for dead. The female who entered the woods with the victim then left with the assailant. Again, the footprints confirm this. As you can see, they circle around and leave with the same patterned boots as before."

"Unlike the female's and the victims boots, the choice of footwear from the attacker is unique isn't it, Jim?" Sarah promoted Jim to add more information.

Jim began to go into detail of the tread and pattern of the attacker's boots. The next slide on the graphic confirmed what Matt, Josh, Helen and Amy were waiting for. Orange boots.

"These boots are one of a kind. They're not overly popular but the designer only made them in an orange colour."

"Do we have anything else?" Sarah quizzed.

"A few things. The police were tidying up a few loose ends this afternoon and they've confirmed that the attacker was wearing a Jolly Hat, also known as a J hat," Jim brought up a still from CCTV by the side of the woods car park, alongside an example of the hat.

"They've got bloody CCTV, you better hope to god that this isn't you," Helen pointed at Matt.

"It's grainy but the police tech team have worked on it. Unfortunately, all you can make out is the hat, a beard and the orange boots. The male completely obscures the female. Admittedly it's not great but we're hoping somebody out there has seen these people and can help with better descriptions."

Jim Jones And Sarah Tunson delved deeper into the surrounding area of Alice Hills. They highlighted an ordnance map of the woods with trail lines showing the footprints of each known person – the dog walker, the victim, the female and the attacker. It turned out that the same dog walker from the start of the woods was the same one to find the body.

The living room was silent. An aura of shock resonated off the walls as the detail of the crime was so close to home. Attacks of this nature are always shocking but the fact it happened on their doorstop made them dwell a bit harder. Helen was getting worried. She knew deep down that Matt wasn't capable of such atrocities, but the law always springs up surprises and Matt's naivety would led him into a trap.

"We and the police believe that the assailant is around six foot tall, broad shouldered and quite physical," Jim added.

Helen glanced over towards Matt, his sleight frame and obvious lack of strength raised a small smile to her tight lips. She was looking more optimistic.

"The skull fracture of the victim is rounded and deep. We believe the weapon to be a baseball bat of some sort and only somebody with brute force could cause such an impact. It is evident from the CCTV and footprints that the female knows the attacker. Was this a premeditated attack? Maybe somebody out there knows?"

"Sorry to interrupt you Jim, but I'm getting some breaking news in my ear," Sarah held the palm of her hand to the earpiece and nodded intensely towards Jim. "They have DNA. They have DNA of the attacker. Unfortunately, this hasn't brought up any matches, but the victim had skin cells of the attacker trapped under his fingernail."

The editors of the TV show updated the graphics board quickly with an outline of a mannequin with a few examples of cuts caused by a deep scratch. Matt pressed his hand against his neck. The fall on the stairs produced a similar scar. Helen looked too, they all looked at Matt as he tried to mask the cut on his neck.

"If we can find a suspect, we're sure that the DNA will prove their guilt. Due to the extent of the cumbersome winter clothing, it is likely that the attacker will have a moderate three inch cut to their face, neck or shoulder," Sarah turned her attention to the camera.

"So, how did you get that cut?" Josh asked Matt.

The TV presenters left contact details on the screen and moved onto the next incident. Matt stood up and made his way to the kitchen again. He clutched his neck further, deep in thought. He had convinced himself that he cut it on the stairs when he fell but now, he was beginning to question himself.

"Talk to us," Helen tried to diffuse Josh's forward question.

They all took the same seats as before and Josh poured everybody bit of wine. His mind was running overtime and he had forgotten that Amy couldn't drink alcohol. She pushed it away with a wry smile. Matt knew that he would be looked at as being crazy but not that he would be looked at as a suspect – especially by his own family.

"You have been acting weird, blacking out and giving details of a crime before anybody else knew about it," Josh paced the kitchen. "Now, it looks like the victim has cut your neck."

"Victim? Who would I attack? This is mad. It started off with as an innocent dream. I only mentioned it because the dream and consequent dreams because they were so vivid." Matt was shaking. "Anyway, they said the person must be big to swing a bat that hard. I'm not big."

"They'll make it fit. They always do," Helen's lip was beginning to quiver.

"Please, please. You have to believe me," Matt could see Helen was getting upset and he rushed around to console her. "You need to believe me."

Matt raised his head and kissed the top of Helen's. Despite his plea, he knew there was always going to be some doubt. He was questioning himself and the others could see that self-suspicion. All of them were addressing him up and down and Matt was beginning to get intimidated. *Is it possible that my elaborate sleep walking could lead me to attack somebody – who was that 'somebody' and why? Could a dream of this intensity leave a physical memoir?* Matt's mind was racing with all sorts of questions.

"You're my family, you're supposed to help and believe me," Matt stuttered, on the verge of crying.

"We believe in you. We love you," Helen reacted with grace.

Josh and Amy seemed sceptical, but they decided to show solidarity as they all embraced Matt. Matt let off a bit of steam by shedding a few tears. It had been years since he had cried, even the funerals of both parents weren't enough to make him cry. He reflected back on his life and couldn't think of a time when he cried – maybe as a teenager when he wasn't 'man' enough.

Matt held the cold tap open for a few seconds before swilling out and filling up a dry glass. The gulps of water offered some time to think about his next steps.

"I'm just going to be quiet about these dreams and hope they go away. I have no enemies, I've no reason to hurt anybody," Matt tried to justify himself but the more he talked about, the more seeds it planted. "Why would the police protect the identity of the victim?"

Nobody replied, they didn't want to argue. Crime Watch and Matt had caused enough damage. A nice meal and a pregnancy reveal had turned sour all because of the television being left on. Matt and Helen were beginning to feel unwelcome, so Matt made his way to the utility room to collect his jacket.

A rounders bat was pinned to the wall to large utility room. *Big Hitter, Champion*, a plaque underlined the beautifully framed bat. Pine coloured with two black stripes – the same as the attacker's bat. Matt checked back to the kitchen, they were all talking amongst themselves, trying to work out a way to help Matt.

The rest of the room was typical of a utility room; washing machine, shoes and laundry. The walls portrayed a different story. Alongside the bat were heaps of trophies and medals. Matt looked at them closely, there must have been close to one hundred trophies. All with the same name. *Amy Stillwell*. Amy was a national rounders player in her younger years and the medals suggested she was also a keen fell runner. The vast number of top medals proved she was good at both. Matt knew she was a competitive sportswoman, a good one too. He just hadn't seen this room or its contents before.

Matt pulled his jacket on and tried to take in more detail of Amy's sporting achievements. He had known Amy for a long time, she was always quiet but confident and determined in life. Stories of her playing days were a common topic of conversation at family get togethers. People need a lot of self-drive to compete at any sport, never mind at national level. Amy had it abundance.

"Are you ok in there?" Josh caught Matt looking at the bat again as he left the utility room.

"Yea, yea. Just thinking."

Matt looked at Amy, glowing and radiant as she caressed her stomach. *Could it be a possibility that she is the attacker?* he thought.

The police confirmed that a bat was involved, and Matt's dream outlined the same description as the one in the utility room. His mind was collating bits of the puzzle together as his narrative began to twist further. The thought lasted two seconds. Matt disgusted himself that he could think like this; he couldn't believe that he was putting his brother's girlfriend in the eye of the storm. Alleging a pregnant woman could do such a thing would be a tough task to put together, even if she did possess a physical talent to swing a bat with force.

Matt needed to defend himself, he was adamant that he did not commit this crime. He zipped up his jacket and closed the utility door behind him. The loose hinge caused the door to crash which attracted the attention of the kitchen to his direction.

"It doesn't look good, I know. I'll visit the station first thing in the morning and explain what I was doing up at Alice Hills. I'd rather look stupid than guilty," Matt stuttered.

"You'll do nothing of the sort. Do not speak to them unless you need to," Helen raged as she knew how the legal world worked.

Thump! Thump! Thump!

"Who is that?!" Helen jumped.

The doorbell was ignored, straight to an obnoxious three-pronged bang to the door. Josh preceded to the corridor but noticed flashing blue lights reflecting off the living room wall. He checked into the living room and looked out of the window. He was greeted to two uniformed police officers glaring through the glass.

"It doesn't look like you'll be going to the police, Matt," Josh laughed as he shouted through to the kitchen. "They've come for you."

Josh had to laugh. Getting each other into trouble always resulted in laughs when they were kids. Just like the time they smashed multiple windows of a house with a football. They blamed each other when confronted by their parents and the police, but no lessons were learnt that day. They rarely were. This time was different, there was a late nervousness to Josh's laugh. A gross and physical attack is higher up the scale than a few smashed windows. He knew this was serious, but he had doubts over Matt's guilt. He just didn't think before opening his mouth.

"What!? No, no, no. This can't be real," Matt was worried as he grabbed Helen.

Helen held Matt close, her usual steely self, had wilted. The walk to the door down the corridor felt like slow motion. Matt was shaking, physically and mentally as a hundred thoughts raced through his head with every step.

"I'll get the door. Just be calm and do not resist. Do what they say," Josh gave some experienced laden instructions as he pushed past to hold the door handle. "You're innocent, we believe you."

Getting into trouble with the police was common with Josh into his late teens, he got involved with a bad crowd and fell for peer pressure. Their dad would be down the station on a regular basis and apologising to neighbours on behalf of Josh. Josh knew what he was doing and that it was wrong. He would often make a conservative effort to keep Matt out of it all. Always the protector.

Helen still had doubts and clutched Matt tighter. Amy held back at the end of the hallway and rubbed her midriff. The commotion wasn't good for her or the baby. She was quiet as usual but looked distressed.

"Don't worry, Amy. Just be calm," Helen reassured her friend and panned back to Matt. "Whatever you do, do not talk in depth about anything until you get a lawyer. I'll get onto John and send him across to the station now."

The perks of working for a high-profile law firm was having the option to pick an expert lawyer at the drop of a hat. John was a criminal lawyer and a close work friend of Helen. He owed her a favour, multiple favours. She had lost count of the amount of times she had contacted his wife to tell her that he would be home late due to a court case over running. When in reality he was out gallivanting with the boys from work.

Matt kissed Helen on the head as Josh pulled the door open. The blue lights lit up the hallway instantly.

"Good evening. Sergeant Morrison and PC Phillips of Alice Hills police," Sergeant Morrison held up her badge.

PC Phillips stood slightly behind Sergeant Morrison's left shoulder with a smarmy smile. The Sergeant had clearly chosen Phillips to help as payback for Matt's earlier introduction at the car park over near the Woods. Both officers made eye contact with Matt, confirming who they were looking for.

"We need to speak to Matthew Crane," Sergeant Morrison stepped into the house, uninvited.

Neither Matt nor the police officers needed to say anything. Everybody knew what it was about. Josh would normally defend his brother under normal circumstances but arguing here wouldn't help the cause.

"**You do not have to say anything**. But, it may harm your defence if **you do not** mention when questioned something which you later rely on in court. **Anything you do say** may be given in evidence," PC Phillips had followed Morrison into the house and clasped the handcuffs on Matt.

Helen needed comfort and switched from the arms of Matt to Josh as the police led Matt outside of the house.

Multiple police vehicles and over ten officers addressed the street. Neighbours were either peering through their curtains or openly gawping from their open front doors with no shame. Matt kept his head down, if his addiction to police TV shows had taught him anything, it was to keep your head down and away from prying eyes and the press. He needed not to worry, there was no press and the neighbours already knew who was in that house.

The night was clear and dry, but the spring cold was bitter as the late hour commenced. He needed the jacket after all.

"Not so smart now, are we?" PC Phillips whispered into his ear as she pressed his head down into the back of the police car.

Matt could do nothing as he sat with his hands cuffed behind his back and his seat belt on. He looked through the window as PC Phillips slammed it shut. The driver barely waited for the door shut before setting off, but Matt got a glimpse of Josh shouting at his neighbours to get back inside. He smirked to himself as he read Josh's lips, 'get inside you nosey bastards'.

Helen had just finished up on the phone to John, "He's on his way to the station."

She rushed to the door but was too late, the last of police cars were long gone.

The silence of the police car was deafening. The officers had turned off their radios. The hum of the car and the passing lights on the road were forcing Matt's eyes to drift. He blinked hard a few times, forcing himself to stay awake.

"Are you ok?" The male driver asked in a husky tone.

The driver was accompanied by PC Phillips who was staring straight ahead into the road. Not so confident without Sergeant Morrison around.

"I'm just tired," Matt replied.

Matt looked up at the mirror and was met with the driver's intense stare. Clean shaven with a chiselled jaw, he filled out the front seat with no room to spare. The physical presence of the driver flicking back and forth between the mirror and the road was enough to keep Matt awake for the rest of the journey.

CHAPTER 8

The car park at Alice Hills police station was large considering the size of its force. A car park space near the door had been left free for the vehicle Matt was traveling in. PC Philips turned her radio on and demanded that somebody escorted the press away from the door before removing Matt from the police car. The blacked-out windows provided secrecy whilst they waited. It was only when the male driver got on the radio and bellowed numerous expletives, that some officers moved the crowd away and around the corner from the main entrance.

PC Philips provided Matt with further confidentiality as she placed a light blanket over his head. Matt stumbled along in the darkness as he was ushered up the steps by a police officer either side of him.

"Get back, get back."

Police officers scrambled to grab a stray photographer. The flashing lights lit dimly through the blanket and caused Matt a little disruption. The clicking noise of the camera seemed to echo from one ear to the other. At least a dozen images were taken before the appeals of free press filtered away into the distance.

Matt noticed the clean white floor as he passed through the automatic door towards the desk. The bright lights of the foyer provided a glow of light around him. The lack of vision heightened other senses; the smell of bleach and beeping sounds of radios and computers muffled out the voices of each officer as they seemed to ponder on what to do next.

Some of the voices began to distort as Matt felt weary. The reality of what was happening was beginning to settle in. His brother had been arrested a few times, but Matt hadn't even had a speeding ticket. Amongst the trepidation, a voice stood out from the crowd. Matt was certain he recognised this voice, but he couldn't put a name to it.

"Look, he's clearly not ready for questioning. He's not all there. Completely out of it."

"Just give him some strong paracetamol and a glass of water," Sergeant Morrison's voice was more obvious.

The blanket was lifted from Matt's head and he was presented with a small plastic cup of water and a couple of tablets. The sudden exposure to light required some eye adjustment, but Matt managed to take the painkillers as his cuffs were taken off.

"Name and address please," the officer at the desk asked.

Matt was surrounded by six officers. He wasn't a fighter; his slim body couldn't fight off one of these officers never mind six. He spun his head left and right which resulted in each officer tensing up, preparing for the worst and eager for Matt to react.

He coughed, "Matthew Crane, 51 Esta Avenue, Alice Hills."

"You are formally advised that you are under arrest for the suspected involvement of an attack on an unnamed male. You are to be questioned and held for up to twenty-four hours."

"OK…"

"Say no more. I need some time with my client, please," Helen's lawyer work friend, John, entered the building.

John Barking was how anybody would imagine a lawyer to look like. A sharp suit matched with a blue tie to advertise his Conservative background. A comb over of gelled hair to the right hand side, teamed with a pair of small glasses. Matt suddenly felt at ease with the presence of a quality lawyer. He had met John several times at family parties and, to his initial surprise, was a down to earth guy. Unlike Helen, he was good at keeping at work life separate from home life and he could adapt his approach to different audiences. He was as a middle class as they come; privately educated and a degree from the best law school in the country. He was always destined for the top but always had time and an interest in others less fortunate.

"You can use the meeting room over here. Five minutes," Sergeant Morrison held the door open for them both.

The door had a strip of glass to the side which allowed the officers to look through. John laid out his briefcase and pulled out a notepad. Still dressed in his zipped up jacket, Matt sat down across the table. John was still in his coat too, he wasn't intending on staying long.

"We need to be quick. It's late and they're going to want to let you stew on your thoughts a bit more," John was confident on the plan.

"But, I didn't do it," Matt explained.

"They don't care about that. Have you seen how quiet it was out there?" John pointed through the window and the officers all looked away. "This is a small crimeless town and they haven't had anything remotely like this. They want a charge against a name. That's all."

"Ok, what shall I do?"

"They're like a child's book, easy to read. They'll ask a few questions and get you in the cell for the night. They'll probably take a DNA sample, I'm happy for you to oblige."

John pointed to a list of police procedural steps on his notepad. It was a well-used list highlighting his confidence on how often this process was used. With each passing word, Matt was gaining more faith. He just hoped that the police system provided the same trust.

"OK, time's up. Come with us," a swift knock by Sergeant Morrison as she held the door open again.

The lobby had dispersed of people. Only the officer at the computer was present as Sergeant Morrison led them to an interview room. The lack of hand cuffs and nonchalant behaviour of the officers was either a clever tactic or stupid behaviour. Maybe some naivety. Either way, it was making Matt overthink things.

"Don't worry, be honest and you'll be fine," John could sense the nervousness.

The interview room was dark and dingy. Just four chairs, two being comfortable and the other two were coffee stained and plastic. The table was basic but bolted to the floor against the wall with a handcuff bar across the middle. Matt looked around the room at the old smoke-stained walls. It was all for intimidation, no upgrades for decades. John on the other hand treated it like a second home. He'd been in rooms like this a thousand times and the way he just slumped himself into the chair without being asked proved that.

"We'll get straight to it," Sergeant Morrison sat across from Matt with PC Phillips beside her.

The recording device was lined up against the wall. It was modern and out of character for the rest of the room. It was a simple record and stop button machine that was linked remotely to the computers on the other side of the wall.

John repeated his process as though it was a motor skill. Briefcase on the table, notes to the side.

They all took a few seconds to get themselves comfortable before Sergeant Morrison commenced recording. A piercing high-pitched tone came from the recorder to introduce the recording. The noise lasted around five seconds and each person at the table looked at one another in the eye as though they were heading into a boxing pre-fight showdown.

"It is twenty-two fifteen on Wednesday January Twenty Five, I'm Sergeant Morrison with PC Phillips in the presence of the suspect, Matthew Crane and his lawyer, John Barking," Sergeant Morrison introduced the group. "For the purpose of this interview, we have recently arrested Mr Matthew Crane on the suspicion of grievous bodily harm against a male victim in the woodland area of Alice Hills at approximately zero six hundred hours on Monday December Ten. The victim's identity is classified."

"My client would like to put on record that he did not commit this crime and denies all involvement," John made his stance clear.

"Well, the information he provided whilst snooping at the crime scene earlier today suggests he knows a fair bit of information. Information that was not officially released until tonight," Morrison explained.

"An inquisitive mind is not evidence, Sergeant. He simply visited the crime scene out of curiosity. He's a local guy with an interest in what goes on his town."

"What do you think, Mr Crane?" PC Philips asked.

Matt looked to John who nodded for him to proceed.

"Remember, this could turn into a homicide case if the victim doesn't pull through from the coma," Sergeant Morrison added.

"I just turned up to see what was going on. It was only whilst I was there that I noticed all of your tape and flags. It painted a good picture for me, and I just worked out the basics of what happened," Matt spurned out an on the spot excuse. "I'm not capable of such a crime, you've got the wrong person."

PC Phillips slid a DNA kit across the table. So far so good, John's prediction was looking positive. It was a small swab enclosed in a plastic tube. She stood up and opened the wrapping.

"We need a DNA sample. You should know the victim scratched the attacker," Phillips looked at the cut on Matt's neck. "We'll have the results tomorrow as we can fast track them. If you are innocent, then you should have nothing to worry about."

"I heard about that on Crime Watch. I'm happy to help."

Holding out the swab, PC Phillips inserted the same into Matt's mouth and swirled it around for ten seconds. Matt brushed his teeth with his tongue as she put the sample into the test tube.

"My client needs to rest. We'll continue this tomorrow when you have the DNA results," John didn't even ask, it was a demand.

"Twenty-Two Twenty, end of interview," Sergeant Morrison pressed stop on the recorder.

The officers were happy, the conversation only lasted five minutes but they gauged Matt's demeanour and got the DNA sample they needed. There would plenty of time for questions if the DNA corresponds positive to the skin cells found under the fingernail of the victim. Morrison and Phillips left the room in a swagger and left Matt and John to talk it over.

"Sometimes you can use the twenty-four-hour timeframe to your own benefit. Rest up and you'll be out of here by the morning," he closed his briefcase. "Don't let them interview you without me."

The door opened and they were both greeted by the uniformed driver who drove the Matt to the station. He was as big as the door frame but gentle as he guided Matt towards the cell. It was late and John wanted to get home. He had been in the law game for so long that he no longer thought about what clients were mentally going through – he presented no sympathy towards Matt and simply left the station like he had just visited a supermarket.

The corridor of blue steel bolted cell doors filled out the next corridor. It was quiet. Matt was going to be alone in the cells tonight. The end cell was the bed of choice, yet another display of psychology games and intimidation from the police but Matt was mindful to it by now. Stories from Helen's cases at work had subconsciously prepared him for all of this.

"Shoes, socks, jacket. Off," the officer demanded as he towered over Matt.

Matt couldn't get them off quick enough. He understood that it was necessary to wear the basics, but suicide was the last thing on his mind. He played along with the police requests just as Helen told him to. *Don't give them a reason keep me here longer than necessary*, he thought.

The door locked behind him as stared down his nose at the single toilet, basic bed and grey blanket. Matt wasn't a well-to-do person but the grimy interior of the cell was worse than he imagined.

"Here's some water. Sleep tight."

The officer passed Matt a polystyrene cup through the hole in the door and then closed it sharply, leaving Matt to his thoughts. The silence of the room echoed his thoughts as though somebody else was in there with him. He necked the drink and lay down under the blanket. The bed wasn't uncomfortable as it looked but it was cold a room. Sleep was the on agenda, it must have been nearing eleven o'clock now and the lack of noise within the room was proving to be a nuisance for Matt's racing thoughts.

Matt went to flip off his shoes as he sat on the edge of bed, already forgetting that the officer had taken them away. His father would be disappointed with him being in a police cell. This was usually Josh's territory; Matt was supposed to be the sensible one. Thinking about his dad led to thoughts about Helen and what she would be doing at home. She would probably be at home now, alone. *I hope she's ok*, he thought.

Part of him still wanted to solve the mystery, an inner demon itching to get out. If the attacker wasn't him in a sleepless state, then who could it be? He was still sure that he was not involved. His head hit the flimsy pillow with a thud against the underside as he pulled across the grey and itchy blanket. The consequences of his actions should have dominated his thoughts but the last thing he thought of before falling asleep was the crime scene.

CHAPTER 9

"Hey, hey. Stop."

Matt with a frantic plea tried his hardest to stop the loving pair from continuing their walk through the woods, but it was to no avail. They couldn't hear him.

Matt looked down and tried to hold out his hands, but he couldn't see himself. It felt different this time, he felt conscious within the dream. The presence seemed real and like an out of body experience as nobody else could see he was there.

A matter of seconds passed as Matt tried to figure out why this time was so different and why he was aware of himself being within the dream. *Focus*, Matt thought to himself. This was a golden opportunity to get ahead. He knew he was asleep, but he couldn't pinpoint where he had fallen asleep. All he knew is that he could be woken up and time was of the essence.

The dog walkers had just passed the couple which prompted Matt to start jogging towards the scene of the attack. Matt couldn't see the arms of his own body as he moved forward. It was a trait of dreams that wouldn't normally be unusual or weird but Matt was conscious of being in the dream so something as odd as his arms re-appearing confused him.

His watch showed the time as seven twenty AM and it was now in working order. He concentrated closely on the faces of the dog walkers and the victims to be but faceless like mannequins blanked him.

Running through the woods allowed for some planning and he decided to try and trace the attacker's steps. The physical exertion was surreal, his heart rate was through the roof and the feeling of sweat was rushing over him. He wiped his forehead to stop the stream of perspiration running into his eyes. Only he couldn't see any of it.

The gate slammed behind him as he left the woods. The car park at the back of woods was empty but he waited in the hope that a car would turn up. The outer area of the car park was blurry; he approached the line between what was visible and the blur and was met with a forcefield. He held out his hand, it was invisible to his eyes, but he could sense the movement of his arm.

Why can't see I anything over here, he thought as his hand pressed to a wall like force. He paced around the car park waiting for car to turn up or at least the attacker to walk by. His dreams had always shown the attacker coming from this direction and the police evidence confirmed it too. Mindful of the time, Matt headed back into the woods. His watch confirmed it was seven twenty-six and he remembered that his watch was broken and stuck at seven thirty in real life. *The attack must happen at seven thirty,* he thought. He guessed that the lovers would be near the crime scene by now.

The gate to the woods was now open but he was sure he slammed this shut on the way out. Matt stretched his back and was perplexed as he looked back over the car park. Footprints were clear to see in the mud which meant he had missed the attacker.

Shit, he thought to himself. *How have I missed him? There is no car.* Matt started to rush through the woods to the scene of the crime, but he was too late.

The victim was lay face down in mud, alone. Matt rushed over to the lifeless body and tried to turn it over. Despite his best efforts, his hands just passed through as though he or the body was a spirit.

He clasped his hands into his face and sighed as he stood up. A mumbling sound could be heard in the background. He looked down at the body but there was no movement, but the mumbling noise happened again. What was being said was hard to decipher, but he peered over to the gate at the back of the woods. It was the attacker and also the lady who was originally with the victim. The jacket of the victim was muddy, but the dark green colour matched that of the woman.

Who are these people and what do they have to do with me, he thought. The attacker had linked arms with the woman and they both reached to one another to kiss. Their faces were obscured but Matt took it upon himself to chase them down. Each forward step that Matt took resulted in no movement. The motion of forward momentum felt real, but the surrounding area didn't move. Matt felt like he was drowning in his own fear and he began to panic. The couple were getting further away, and no progress had been made, despite the different outlook on the dream.

"Urrghh."

The body on the floor began to move as the grumble echoed through the woods. The gate of the woods slammed shut. The assailant and his partner hadn't heard the victim, they presumed that he was dead. Matt knelt down as the body had managed to turn over onto its back. There was no face, just a beard with no other features. Matt circled the face as more groans came from the victim's direction but nothing. No outline of a jaw or eyebrow line.

"He's here. He's alive and awake. Quick!"

The voice came from the opposite side of the wooded area and the tone of the appeals sounded like somebody had found the body.

Matt had lost track of time and his watch was stuck at seven thirty. He was sure that the couple had only just left the scene, so he was left wondering how the dog walker had already turned up with the police and medical services. He pushed himself up from the sodden ground to check the perimeter. The surrounding ten metre radius showed no signs of anybody approaching. More groans came from the faceless victim and Matt could do nothing but wander around as an invisible body. Frustration was setting in as he panned the boundary of trees for a sign of the dog walker and any police officer. He could hear them clearly but visually there was nothing, but the writhing of the victim was in the woods.

Then a small rustle in earshot of Matt's position caught his attention.

"Hey, Hey. You. Over here. Listen up," the voice was coarse but nobody could be seen.

CHAPTER 10

Matt woke up on the floor in a pool of sweat next to the bed of the prison cell. The grey itchy blanket was strewn across the room and he was clutching the polystyrene cup.

"Hey, Hey. You. Over here. Listen up," an officer shouted through the police cell window.

Matt pushed his back against the wall and pressed his hands into his face. He could see his legs were intact, "Yea, what's up?"

"I'll leave this drink and food here. You've got twenty minutes before your lawyer gets here."

Matt lifted himself up and staggered over to the door to grab the tray that was balancing within the window of the door. The plate of food looked appetising, much nicer than what Helen could prepare. Not that Matt would ever say such a thing to her face. The bones of his buttocks pressed into the solid concrete like bed. Shuffling around made no difference but tucking into the hospital style food made up for the lack of comfort.

The dream provided a slightly different perspective for Matt but he still couldn't work out what he was supposed to do. The blank canvass of the police cell provided no inspiration and the shouts from a local drunk in the next cell clouded his mind further. Plus he was feeling more anxious as Helen was probably wondering where he was.

The sound of a key turn resonated off the four walls and the steel door opened wide. The voice of a drunk male became louder but it wasn't clear what he was shouting about.

"You're up. Your man is early," a lone female officer held the door ajar.

Matt scoffed the remaining morsels of his food left and jumped to his feet. He was feeling optimistic; the latest dream wasn't evidence, but it gave him personal assurance that he wasn't the attacker.

The large officer from yesterday met Matt at the door, the female wasn't alone after all. He handed Matt his clothes and shoes and told him to freshen up.

"Have you been home yet?" Matt tried to lighten the mood, but he didn't reply.

Atop of the clothes was a damp flannel and a self-lubricated toothbrush so getting cleaned up and dressed was a quick process. He didn't want to stay in the cell a minute longer anyway so he rubbed down his face and hands, and threw the remains onto the bed.

The groans and demands of the alcohol fuelled idiot were clearer as Matt passed the neighbouring cell.

"Just ignore him; he's a regular," the female officer banged on the door of the cell, "Shut up!"

"Get me out of here. I'm ill and this is like a prison," the drunk shouted the last sentence repeatedly.

"He really is drunk eh. Doesn't even know where he is," Matt laughed.

Matt checked in his personal details again at the main desk before meeting his lawyer, John Barking, in the interview room.

"Looking rough," John was blunt. "It'll be quick again. They'll have the DNA results, but they'll drag it out a bit. Just listen to what they have to say, and you'll be out of here in no time."

"Are you that confident?" Matt stroked his unshaven gristly chin.

"Always. I've spoken to Helen and she is on her way."

Matt had no reason to disbelieve him. He was spot on yesterday and Matt absorbed the confidence from John.

PC Phillips and Sergeant Morrison entered the room. They were both determined to see this through together. The room was relaxed, Matt had been treated with respect for the whole of his stay at the station. John, Matt and the officers took the same seats as yesterday and sat across from each other.

Sergeant Morrison took a moment to flick through her paperwork and prepare herself. She licked her finger before turning each page, trying to build some tension.

"Come on," John wasn't impressed with the time wasting.

PC Phillips pulled the TV screen over to the table. Neither John or Matt had noticed the TV set on the way in. The room was bare so it should have stood out like a sore thumb.

"It is eight zero seven on January Twenty Six. I'm Sergeant Morrison with PC Phillips in the presence of the suspect, Matthew Crane and his lawyer, John Barking," Sergeant Morrison introduced the group just like yesterday and checked her watch.

"Do you sleepwalk often, Matt?" PC Philips reached over to the TV and turned it on.

"Sometimes."

Matt couldn't elaborate any further as a copy of some CCTV flashed up on the screen and grabbed his attention.

"For the purpose of the tape, we are showing CCTV footage of Matt's overnight stay in the cell last night," Sergeant Morrison sat back in her chair.

The footage was sped up on a time lapse, but it was obvious what was occurring. Matt watched himself pace the prison cell room left, right and centre. He could envisage himself within the dream again as he cross referenced the footage – left at the bed, left at the gate within the woods, crouching down in the cell, crouching down to the body. The prison cell couldn't have been any bigger than three metres squared but Matt was matching every step exactly to that of his dream. The kneeling down to the victim was clear to see, not that anybody else in the room could tell what he was doing.

"Care to explain that?" Sergeant Morrison leant forward towards Matt as the video tape concluded.

Matt knew what she was insinuating. His family had already suggested that he could possibly do drastic things in his sleep. Maybe they were all right. Matt thought back, he couldn't remember any of this or any previous sleep walking incidents. Sleep attacks were something of fantasy. Something he had seen on late night American TV programmes.

"Can you even link me to the victim? What motive do I allegedly have?" Matt said frustratingly. "Who is the victim?"

John was taken aback by Matt's outrage. Matt blushed a little, even he was surprised at his snap reaction. It was completely out of character and John knew this. Helen always described Matt as the laid-back type of guy, but every man has his breaking point.

"We cannot delve more info on the victim. We've said this numerous times over the past couple of days and relayed the same to the media," Sergeant Morrison replied with the same sort of frustration.

"But surely you should know if I have a link to this victim?" Matt was exasperated as he flapped his hands in the air.

"Look, we're obviously not going into detail as my client is innocent. You know that, we know that," John pointed to the unsealed envelope sat in front of PC Phillips. "Reopen it, I can see you've already read it so why are we going on this weird goose chase."

PC Phillips tapped the envelope up and down on the desk and sighed as she looked across to Matt. The police force still needed to conduct an interview but again, the naivety of an inexperienced police station came to the fore. Sergeant Morrison hadn't noticed the envelope on the way into the interview room and showed an obvious face of disgust as she shook her head towards her young colleague.

Not for the first time, and unlikely to be the last, PC Phillips was left embarrassed. Only this time, there was nowhere to go.

"It's not a full DNA match," Sergeant Morrison had no alternative but hand over the envelope.

"Thank you. Me and my client would like to leave you to carry on with your investigation," John sarcastically said. "A formal complaint with regards to your conduct will be filed in due course."

"End of interview," Sergeant Morrison turned off the recording device without a proper sign off.

Matt hadn't felt relief like this before. A surge of adrenaline rushed through his body as he headed to the door with his lawyer. John's instinct was second to none. Knowledge, experience and confidence. He had it all and played a simple yet effective game. Matt didn't have to speak about his dreams and make a potential fool of himself. He was grateful for Helen's choice of lawyer.

"Helen is on her way. Say hi from me when she picks you up," John patted Matt on the back and left him at the desk to collect his personal belongings.

"Cheers John, I owe you one."

"I'll bill Helen," John laughed and raised his briefcase to wave goodbye as he left through the automatic door.

Matt stuffed his wallet, phone and keys into his pockets and left the building without saying another word. The smell of fresh hit him as if he had been locked up for weeks. *NOT A MATCH*, he read the letter in his head and held it up against sun. Matt squinted his eyes as though to check the authenticity of the letter, it was watermarked at least.

Treating the letter like a prized possession, he slowly folded it up along the preformed lines and sealed the envelope shut. John was still here somewhere. His Bentley, brand new and shining with a private registration plate, was a dead giveaway in a near empty car park. Matt started to walk around the car park in search for Helen's car but it was John that he spotted first. He was bent over leaning into a car and laughing. Matt now spotted Helen's car.

Helen beeped her horn unnecessarily, but she was excited to see her husband and clambered out of her car and nearly knocked John over in the process. John took no offence and waved goodbye for a second time before heading to his car.

"I'm sorry, I'm sorry," Helen had a real sympathetic tone to her voice.

Matt held the envelope in the air to avoid creasing it as Helen grabbed hold of Matt and kissed him. Their eyes locked before they kissed again, being together for so many years brought an element of telepathic ability. They knew they didn't need to explain their prior reactions.

"My letter of freedom," Matt opened the letter as though he was a proud schoolboy with a good report.

"I know. Great news, John told me everything," she pushed the letter away. "Come on, let's get some breakfast."

"Can we get a rain check on that, I'm shattered," Matt yawned. "I just want a few hours in my own bed."

"Sure. I love you, you know," Helen twisted her arm into Matt's and turned towards their car.

"Love you too."

CHAPTER 11

The day was already beginning to look bright. It was spring but the air was slightly warm in a cloudless sky. This only perked Matt up more as he sat in the passenger with a smug smile on his face.

"I'm absolutely knackered," Matt stretched his neck.

"I'm not surprised, those beds are like concrete."

"So is the floor."

"I don't want to ask. I'm just glad we've got you home."

Helen concentrated her attention back to the road, but Matt could see a glint in her eye. He felt young again, as if the pair of them had only just met.

"I need to say this, it's been eating away at me," Helen coughed to clear her throat. "I'm sorry I didn't believe you."

"Don't worry. It's done. I just hope these dreams stop now," Matt interrupted Helen.

They both had a deep feeling that the dreams would continue. Matt was free but so was the attacker. The attacker is out there somewhere, and the police seemed to have put all their efforts into tailing Matt.

"It's a bit worrying that the police went after you. I can see why they did it as you turned up at the crime scene with details of the crime," Helen could laugh now as she pulled into the driveway.

"I played into their hands. They clearly don't have any other leads," Matt replied. "Let's forget about it now. Let me have a couple of hours sleep and we'll head out for lunch."

"You can have a shower before you get into our bed. You smell awful."

Home sweet home, it had only been a night away but a little jibe like that from Helen was what Matt needed to appreciate his life. His body was completely drained as he struggled to climb the stairs with his lack of energy. His mind was the complete opposite. Each step on the staircase accentuated an exaggerated body motion onto the next step. The grip on the handrail tightened harder as he progressed to the top.

"Are you ok? I'll follow you up," Helen could see the struggle and pressed up behind Matt.

"Yea, I just feel really alert. It feels like everything is getting brighter and my focus is more intense."

"That'll be the adrenaline. You will be high off it," Helen put her hand around Matt's waist and focussed her attention to his eyeline. "Your nose. It's bleeding."

Matt raised his right hand towards his nose. Now that it had been drawn to his attention he started to feel the gradual flow of blood drip onto his upper lip. He splayed the fingers and palm of his hand to assess the damage. There was no blood on his hand. He rubbed the back of his hand around nose and checked again. Nothing. His hand was clean.

"What are you doing?" exclaimed Helen as she used the sleeve of her top to stem the stream of blood on Matt's nose.

"There's nothing there," Matt stopped in his tracks as he looked into the mirror at the top of the stairs.

He glanced back and forth to his hand and reflection in the mirror. He had smeared blood all over his face and hand, but he could only see this within the mirror.

"Just stay still whilst I wipe this down," Helen dabbed Matt's nose with a flannel she had retrieved from the bathroom. "It looks like it has stopped, jump in the shower now. You smell awful."

Matt reluctantly agreed but he was starting to get a searing headache as he turned on the shower. He stripped down and stared closely and intently into the bathroom mirror. His peripheral vision was blurry, and he noticed his pupils had shrunk to pinpoint dots.

Helen's footsteps could be heard heading back downstairs. She had left Matt to his own devices and knew that the bedrest would be all he needed. But Matt was swaying in the shower and he was struggling to stand. Sensing the danger and remembering previous black outs, he cleaned up quick and slumped onto the bed, still wet.

"Are you ok?" Helen shouted from downstairs.

"Yea, wake me up in a couple of hours," Matt croaked.

The room began to spin as Matt stared towards the ceiling. His wet hair had dampened the bed and his body didn't seem to be getting any drier. Each blink of his eyes sped up the tempo of the room rotation. The light wasn't on and the curtains were still closed from this morning, but the room got brighter and brighter with each passing second. Closing his eyes didn't stop the brightness, nor did it stop the spinning, and the revolutions of the room eventually knocked him unconscious.

CHAPTER 12

The crunch of the dry leaves amongst the squelch of mud was unmistakable. Matt was back in the woods and in the presence of the loving pair as they linked arms and gazed into one another's eyes.

He looked down at himself and couldn't see his hands or body. An invisible force again and Matt felt physically present but useless knowing what was coming. The pair continued their stroll as the dog walker past them. Matt followed behind them. Knowing how the story panned out, he spent the time astonished at how real it all felt. His soul was there, and he could feel the crisp wind against his imageless face. The footsteps he was taking weren't leaving prints but there was a sinking feeling in the mud adding to the physical presence he was experiencing.

.The gait of the victim and the woman wasn't unique. They could be anyone. Each step they took was in sync and they were clearly in love as the gently pushed each other back and forth between laughter. Matt stared ahead, he felt like he couldn't gain any more detail than what he already knew so decided to let the dream take its course. Their faces were still obscured. The voices were clear but monotone. Similar to the walking style, there was nothing distinctive about their voices.

Is this dream trying to steer me or send me a message? Matt thought to himself. The previous dreams encouraged him to investigate anything and everything. This current dream was making him get all philosophical about it. Thoughts and ideas were running through his mind, distracting him from where he was walking.

The couple had stopped in their tracks and Matt could not react in time. Despite the lack of his physical presence he still reacted as he would in real life by trying to stop. It was too late and his consciousness immersed into the body of the male.

Matt felt trapped and he couldn't move back and forth. He tried to raise his hands and move his feet but his presence had been completely absorbed into the body of the male. Looking around on a pivot was fine and he looked up and down before glancing left towards the female. The conversation between the pair continued to flow and Matt was a sitting parasite as he was forced to listen about nonsensical subjects.

"I've told Josh about the pregnancy," the female voice, still obscured, turned towards the male and stopped him in his tracks.

Josh? As much as Matt tried, he couldn't make out the face of the female. He was perplexed, this conversation hadn't taken place previously. The conversation of having children was a topic Matt had heard in the previous dreams, but the mention of a name hadn't.

The atmosphere had taken a remarkable turn and Matt was fixated on the female. *Who is this woman and why is she telling Josh that she's pregnant?* The lack of control Matt had was irritating him but all he could do was sit and listen, not without taking his eye off the female.

"What did he say?" the male replied as they continued to walk.

"He's ecstatic. He thinks that it's his baby."

"Well, is it?"

"It has to be. We've been struggling for a long time now and all the tests show that he has a low sperm count," she looked down to the ground before lifting her head towards the eyeline of the male.

Amy? It's Amy, she's talking about Josh, as soon as Matt processed the name in his mind the face of the female started to transpire. There was an awkward interaction between them as the face of the female became Amy. Matt felt liked he had been spotted within the dream, like a ghost; the eye contact felt real as they stared at one another.

Matt was engrossed in the conversation. He was in the body of the victim and unless his mind was playing tricks with him, the female was Amy. The scene of the attack was approaching, Matt could see the fallen tree in the distance and knowing the assault was imminent, it triggered some anxiety. This dream started off without any hope, but huge progress had been made in a matter of a few minutes and Matt's anxiety had an element of excitement.

The conversation got back to the recognisable flow as the attacker approached from up ahead. Nothing had changed here; the mist had opened up, and the outline of the looming male was beginning to emerge. A faceless beard, the attacker, passed the pair and disappeared into the distance.

Matt could do nothing but go along for the ride, mummified in the body of the future victim. He watched Amy jump the tree, but he couldn't turn to try an locate the attacker – his neckline had locked with that of the victim.

The anticipation was unbearable as Matt braced himself for the impending impact. He couldn't remember the exact second the strike was going to happen and even though his physical body wasn't there he tensed ready for impact.

Thud!

Matt instantly blacked out and fell into an abyss of darkness. There was no pain, there was no feeling of the bat striking the back of the head.

Curdling screams shrieked through the air as the eyesight of the victim started to materialise. A profound cloud began to disperse as the victim dropped in and out consciousness. Matt followed every phase of the victim with no control.

"Why? Why? Get up, get up," Amy rushed over to lift the flailing body.

In between the lifelessness, Matt knew that the attacker was coming over to take Amy away. He just hoped that the brief intervals of vision would show who it was.

"Help!" Amy let out a scream.

"Be quiet," a male voice muttered.

"What? What are you doing here?" Amy replied. "I think you've killed him."

"Well, I can't do anything now. I can't touch him; I might leave evidence."

The attack had taken Amy by surprise. Matt knew the attacker was familiar to Amy as he knows they walk away from the scene together.

"Just one second," Amy was hysterical as she bent down towards the body.

"Did you not think I'd find out about your sordid little affair?" The attacker was outraged.

Matt could hear everything clearly, but the range of vision was limited to the victim's perception. *Who are these guys that Amy has gotten involved with?* He thought.

"We need to go now," the male attacker tried to lift Amy up to her knees.

"Matt..." Amy didn't have chance to elaborate and was lifted up to walk away from the scene by the attacker.

It took a moment, but Matt began to phase into the body of the victim completely. The penetrating pain to the back of head was severe enough to limit body functions. Matt was the victim and began to take control of the body and feel every ounce of pain. It was limited movement but he managed to turn his head in the direction of Amy and the attacker as they walked towards the gate of the woods.

The woods provided a second of silence and at the same time, Amy and the attacker turned to face Matt for one last time. Blood streamed down Matt's face and dripped off the edge of his eyelashes, but the face of the attacker was clear.

"Josh," Matt croaked.

The voice was his own and that of the body. It was all he could muster up in his paralytic state as he dribbled blood into the muddy ground.

"He's here. He's alive and awake. Quick!"

Matt drifted in and out of consciousness, but he heard the voice of the dog walker and knew help was on the way and relaxed into a deep sleep.

CHAPTER 13

"That's it. We're here, he's coming around."

A distinctive voice rang in the distance. The pitch black images brightened slowly and began to contrast towards a shade of white. Matt focussed on the pocket of white light and headed towards it. The same, unknown voice called out his name over and over, it was resonating from the glowing orb. A beam of light, like a torch, got larger the closer Matt moved towards it – or was the light approaching Matt? The sense of disassociation and walking on air puzzled Matt. The surrounding area was pitch black and he couldn't physically feel his body moving, only his mind, as though he was gravitating towards the light.

"Matt. Please."

Another plea came from the direction of the ever-brightening light. Matt recognised the voice this time. *Helen*. His mind was the only present entity that he could sense but he suddenly felt a physical squeeze of his hand. He set out to move faster but he couldn't press forward. As much as he tried, the pace of movement remained the same. As though he was on an escalator going the wrong way.

Am I dying? Am I not waking up from my sleep? Matt thought back to the shower and him falling asleep on the bed. His last memory was falling on asleep on the bed after a night in the police cell. Oddly, his dream was clearer than the detail leading up to it.

The white light intensified, and Matt began to get sensitive to it. A burning sensation rushed over him as the darkness dispersed into light.

Beep, beep, beep.

Matt felt his hand being squeezed again and the whiteness of the light filtered slowly to reality. A brief blur of vision turned to sharp focus as his eyes blinked and rolled back and forth.

"Helen?" Matt croaked.

"Get a doctor. He's awake!" Helen screamed.

Matt tried to pry both of his eyes open but only one eye was giving sight. He lifted a limp left hand towards his head and felt a bandage wrapped around his head and across his left eye. His hand draped down and across his neck where he was met with another bandage leading into his shoulder. He was aching and he could barely his move body. The beeping machine and wires hooked up to his body told him he was in hospital.

He blinked several times to help focus as he looked at Helen, she was exhausted yet radiant. The hospital ward was bland, but Matt noticed that the colours of the room were vibrant and clearer than ever. He grabbed Helen's hand. It felt real as he caressed and gripped it.

"Where am I? Have I had brain surgery?"

Matt's only assumption was that his weary ways and graphic dreams was a result of an underlying tumour of some sort. The bandage across his head led to him think of the worst-case scenario.

"You're at the Great Northern Hospital. Take it easy, a doctor is on the way," Helen kissed Matt on the cheek.

"My dreams and my blackouts. Have I had some sort of fit?"

"What? I think the drugs are still in your system. You were attacked in Alice Hills woods," Helen kept an eye on the heart rate monitor. "You've been in a coma for four days."

The doctor entered the room, Josh and Amy followed her in. All of the focus turned to the doctor. She was short, and slender with a strong posture. Her routine was regimented, as she started out by checking Matt's clipboard and vitals at the end of the bed. Apart from the machines, the room was quiet, and everybody had taken a seat, gawping at Matt and the doctor, waiting for some positive news.

"Matt. My name is Dr Qureshi. How are you feeling?" she spoke softly and pressed the button on the bed keypad to raise the mattress at a slight incline.

Matt tried to force himself to sit up in the bed but struggled. He was disorientated, stiff and the drugs were limiting his movements.

"I guess I'm ok?" Matt questioned himself. "Alive at least... I think."

The reality of it all wasn't settling in with Matt. One moment he was falling asleep on his bed at home, then he was dreaming about the crime. And now he's woken up from a coma in a hospital bed.

"You're far from okay but the fact you're awake and talking is a huge positive," she lifted his shirt and pressed a stethoscope into his chest.

The doctor pulled a small light and tilted Matt's eyes back. One at a time, she checked the pupils of Matt's dreary eyes. It triggered a memory from the car chase and the headlights going from one eye to the other. The length time on the eye checks lasted a matter of seconds in reality but the flashback to car chase did a five-minute speed run though Matt's mind. He lay back in the hospital bed as he vividly remembers being chased by a car with Helen as the passenger – the head lights of the chasing car reflected through the central mirror and blinded Matt, one eye at a time.

Matt felt his arm and noticed that a drip was connected, looking up at the bag heightened the noise of the water dripping through to the tube. Flash backs to all of the dripping sounds from the shower at home flicked his mind.

Matt looked over to Helen for moral support as a tried to piece things together, "I can feel my legs and feet too." He clenched his fists slowly; double checking how real things were.

"Everything looks promising," Dr Qureshi had checked over Matt. "We still need to some more scans, especially now that you're awake. You've taken a huge trauma to the head and it's likely you'll be here for a while."

"How long? What's wrong with me?" Matt tried to shuffle up the bed.

"Try to stay still and rest," Dr Qureshi pressed the button on the bed to raise the gradient and tilt Matt to a forty-five-degree angle.

"Do you not remember anything?" Helen had moved from her chair to comfort Matt.

"I fell asleep on our bed after a shower and then I've woken up here," he licked his dry lips. "I was in the police station the night before, remember?"

Amy looked at Helen in bewilderment and Josh followed suit. Dr Qureshi took a step back and they were all a bit puzzled and thought Matt was a bit disorientated.

"You don't remember getting attacked?" Josh asked and opened a polystyrene case of food.

The smell of school type dinners from Josh's lap hit Matt instantly. Again, it triggered a flash back to when Matt pulled onto his driveway and could smell the same sort of food for no apparent reason.

"What?" Josh stopped and mumbled with a mouthful of food as Matt stared at him.

"Nothing. Nothing," Matt shook his head and refocused. "So, you know about my dreams? You don't think I'm crazy?"

"Nobody is crazy in hospital. We're to help," Dr Qureshi replied.

"Get me out of here. I'm ill and this is like a prison," Just on cue, a random voice was hheard shouting from the next room.

"Ignore him, it's just some drunk," Josh added.

Matt clearly remembered that voice and sentence from the prison cell. He took a deep breath to compose himself and took in a smell of lavender from the nearby flowers.

"They're from me," Helen laughed as she rearranged the flowers. "You smell awful and need a shower, but the lavender helps."

Matt laughed but creased at the pain. He suddenly remembered the numerous times over the past few days that Helen was forcing him into the shower because of his bad smell. The lavender bed sheets were also a prominent memory.

"Anyway, dreams? What dreams? You were found in Alice Hills after an attack. No dreams played a part in this," Helen brushed her hand on Matt's.

"I don't understand," Matt was in pain and hugely confused on what was going on.

"Monday. You went for an early walk through the woods. Somebody has hit you on the back of the head with a bat and left you for dead," Helen touched the bandages around his around head softly. "You were with somebody, but nobody knows who and that same somebody left the scene with the person who attacked you."

Josh stood up with a plastic cup of water and handed it to Matt. He slid next to Helen and comforted her.

"You don't remember anything," Josh put it bluntly, a statement or question? Matt couldn't quite decide.

"It's national news. They've released bits of CCTV and small clues like what the attacker was wearing. But they have no leads, they're basically waiting for you."

"Have you been here the whole four days talking about it?" Matt asked.

"Pretty much. The police always gave updates here at the hospital. We were sure you could hear us. Your eyes flickered a lot, you mumbled and had slight fits of movement," said Helen.

"Yea, Sergeant Morrison was beginning to piss us off. She was wanting to interview you even though you were half dead," Josh got agitated just at the thought.

"Even the in-laws have been here. You know, for moral and loving support," Josh added. "It cramped the room a bit and the doctors weren't happy, but you showed real signs of life on that day."

"The Fentanyl," Matt whispered to himself, or so he thought.

"Yea, they pumped you with loads of drugs. You'd sweat like a maniac but the doctors reassured us that it was fine," Josh flicked the water drip and laughed.

Another flashback and Matt began to start to realise the truth of what was going on. He remembered taking the Fentanyl in physical form before going into his living room and seeing the in-laws. The confusion on Matt's face loosened as things started to become clear.

Matt peered around to look at Amy sat alone on the chair. She was rubbing her stomach in a circular motion.

"Are you…"

"Well, we wanted to wait until you were out of here," Josh pulled Amy up from the seat and put his arm around her back. "But yea, we're having a baby."

Helen let out a little scream but immediately apologised in the direction of Matt as he winced. The news of Matt coming around from a coma and now Amy being pregnant was turning the day into a great day for Helen.

"We've been struggling for a while but bang it just happened," Josh was clearly happy.

Suddenly, Matt started to realise that he had dreamed everything whilst in a coma. The sublevel dreams within the coma all made sense. A dream within a dream. *No wonder I knew so much about the attack*, he thought to himself. The headlights from the car chase was really the doctor conducting a check-up. All the sweating and heart rate increases, the smelling of hospital food, the weird conversations without responses, family meetings and visions of him in a hospital gown - it all began to make sense to Matt.

Matt looked Josh square in the eyes. He knew he was the attacker. Josh gulped as the eye contact got unbearably long. Josh eventually looked away and sat back down with Amy. Amy replicated Josh's expression as she nestled back into her seat.

"Who were you out with walking with?" Helen asked.

Matt checked back over to the Josh and Amy. He knew the chances of the baby being his were high but, Josh clearly thought it was his. Being struck with a near fatal blow by his own brother didn't sit well but having an affair with his brother's girlfriend meant it was an expected reaction. Matt was sure that Josh only knew it was Matt having the affair with Amy after the attack. He could never imagine Josh nearly killing him, no matter what the circumstances. Josh was an erratic guy, and it wouldn't be beyond him to have had an inkling of an affair and instantly tail Amy on the first thought of it.

The idea of telling Helen the truth; the fact he was having an affair with Amy and he could be the dad of the unborn baby, did cross his mind. The dream gave a small glimpse of what would happen if the truth came out. Josh would be charged and probably sent to prison, and the family would be ripped apart for good. He remembered his dad's dying words that the family needed to stick together.

Josh leant forward and took a deep breath; clearly worried that Matt was going to tell all to Helen. Amy mimed the word *please* behind Josh's back in the direction of Matt. The consequences of the truth were too great. Matt had always wanted to be a dad and Amy was more than likely carrying his child so the temptation was there, but the bigger picture came to the forefront of Matt's mind. Josh and Amy would be great parents and Helen would be devasted at this sort of mistrust.

"I don't remember. I don't remember who I was with or why somebody would attack me," Matt smiled at Helen. "We'll just have to hope the police find them."

Josh could hold the secret of his brother and Amy's affair and Matt was happy to share the load. The signals between Josh and Amy suggested that Amy had told him that the baby was his and the affair was nothing but a short fling.

"Not to worry. We're all just glad to have you back," Helen looked at Josh and Amy.

"Definitely, we'll have a big party when you're back home," Josh laughed. "We'll leave you both to it for a bit. Come on Amy let's grab a drink."

Helen waited for the door to firmly close and placed her hands against Matt's cheeks. Looking into her eyes, Matt could see real love. She didn't know about the affair.

"I've realised that life is too short. I think we should start trying for a family."

Matt's eyes lit up but the smile triggered a small shooting pain in his head and he grimaced.

"I'm sorry," Helen kissed Matt. "I know I work too much, so it's time I started to focus on homelife over work life."

Matt was guilty of a big wrongdoing. He was married, Amy wasn't, but cheating on his wife with his brother's girlfriend was borderline criminal. Despite this, and Josh attacking him, he felt positive. His body would eventually heal, and he'd be out of the hospital soon. Amy and Josh were going to be parents and Helen was prepared to give Matt the gift of parenthood too.

"Let's make this work," he hugged Helen with an overpowering feeling of guilt.

Printed in Poland
by Amazon Fulfillment
Poland Sp. z o.o., Wrocław